Luke Chu[...]
Sound Caused Maggie To Shiver

"Are you cold?" Luke said, pulling her even closer.

Maggie's breasts were crushed to the hard wall of Luke's chest in a sweet pain that made her acutely aware of her femininity in contrast to his blatant maleness.

"No. I'm—I'm definitely not cold."

"You feel so good in my arms, Maggie. Perfect, absolutely perfect."

"Well…" Maggie started, then for the life of her couldn't think of one intelligent thing to say.

And the music played on.

Dear Reader,

Celebrate the conclusion of 2005 with the six fabulous novels available this month from Silhouette Desire. You won't be able to put down the scintillating finale to DYNASTIES: THE ASHTONS once you start reading Barbara McCauley's *Name Your Price*. He believes she was bought off by his father…she can't fathom his lack of trust. Neither can deny the passion still pulsing between them.

We are so excited to have Caroline Cross back writing for Desire…and with a brand-new miniseries, MEN OF STEELE. In *Trust Me,* reunited lovers have more to deal with than just relationship troubles—they are running for their lives. Kristi Gold kicks one out of the corral as she wraps up TEXAS CATTLEMAN'S CLUB: THE SECRET DIARY with her story of secrets and scandals, *A Most Shocking Revelation.*

Enjoy the holiday cheer found in Joan Elliott Pickart's *A Bride by Christmas,* the story of a wedding planner who believes she's jinxed never to be a bride herself. Anna DePalo is back with another millionaire playboy who finally meets his match, in *Tycoon Takes Revenge.* And finally, welcome brand-new author Jan Colley to the Desire lineup with *Trophy Wives,* a story of lies and seduction not to be missed.

Be sure to come back next month when we launch a new and fantastic twelve-book family dynasty, THE ELLIOTTS.

Melissa Jeglinski

Melissa Jeglinski
Senior Editor
Silhouette Books

Please address questions and book requests to:
Silhouette Reader Service
U.S.: 3010 Walden Ave., P.O. Box 1325, Buffalo, NY 14269
Canadian: P.O. Box 609, Fort Erie, Ont. L2A 5X3

Joan Elliott Pickart

A Bride by Christmas

Silhouette® Desire

Published by Silhouette Books
America's Publisher of Contemporary Romance

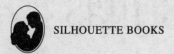 SILHOUETTE BOOKS

ISBN 0-373-76696-3

A BRIDE BY CHRISTMAS

Copyright © 2005 by Joan Elliott Pickart

This edition published by arrangement with Harlequin Books S.A.

® and TM are trademarks of Harlequin Books S.A., used under license.
Trademarks indicated with ® are registered in the United States Patent
and Trademark Office, the Canadian Trade Marks Office and in other
countries.

Visit Silhouette Books at www.eHarlequin.com

Printed in U.S.A.

JOAN ELLIOTT PICKART

is the author of over one hundred books. When she isn't writing, Joan enjoys reading, needlework, gardening and attending craft shows on the town square. She has all-grown-up daughters as well as a young daughter, Autumn, who is in elementary school. Joan, Autumn, and a three-pound poodle named Willow live in a charming small town in the high pine country of Arizona.

For all the lovely ladies at Willow Wind

One

Luke St. John walked slowly up the wide steps leading to the porch, and the carved wooden doors of the large Episcopal church. He stopped at the doors, marveling at their intricate craftsmanship.

It really was a majestic structure, he thought, and he could understand why his brother and Ginger had chosen to be married here tomorrow. The event had been many months in the planning, and Robert had confided that Ginger had changed her mind about colors and endless other details so many times the wedding coordinator must be ready to strangle his bride-to-be.

Luke smiled as he opened one of the doors and entered the vestibule.

Ginger Barrington, he mused, was an endearing yet

rather ditzy young woman who had been given a blank check by her father to have the wedding of her dreams. The last he'd heard, Ginger had chosen seven brides-maids for the don't-worry-about-the-cost event.

Whatever. The people in the Barrington-St. John social circle were accustomed to these kinds of extravaganzas. What was important was that Ginger and Robert were deeply in love—and they were, they really were.

Strange, Luke thought. He'd actually felt a twinge of envy on more than one occasion as he'd watched the relationship between Robert and Ginger develop. He'd been startled each time he'd registered that green-around-the-edges feeling. He dated independent career women and that suited him just fine. But then again…

Luke shook his head to halt his jumbled thoughts and glanced at his watch.

He was early for the rehearsal, he knew, but a business meeting on this side of town had ended sooner than expected. There wasn't time to go home, nor any point in returning to the office, so he'd come here with the idea of sitting in the quiet church and relaxing until the others arrived.

Luke crossed the vestibule, entered the large sanctuary, then walked down the aisle past about a dozen pews to finally settle onto one. He swept his gaze over the high ceiling and exquisite stained-glass windows, nodding again in approval.

His attention was caught by a side door opening close to the altar. A woman entered carrying a cardboard box. His gaze was riveted on her as she crossed to the center aisle and placed the box on the first pew, immediately removing a large yellow satin bow.

Luke felt a sudden pain in his chest and drew a sharp breath as he realized he hadn't breathed since the woman had appeared. He leaned forward, resting his arms on the rail in front of him, and drank in the sight of her, missing no detail.

She was so beautiful, Luke thought rather hazily. No, that wasn't the word he wanted. Beautiful was what the career women he dated strove for, which resulted in cookie-cutter perfection in clothes, hair and makeup that varied little from one to the next.

No, this woman, who was now attaching the satin bow to the side of the first pew was…pretty. Yes, that was the word. Pretty in a wholesome, breath-of-fresh-air way that was knocking him for a loop. She was sunshine on a cloudy day, real, what-you-see-is-what-you-get real, and he'd bet ten bucks she wasn't wearing any makeup at all.

Her strawberry-blond hair tumbled to her shoulders in what he was convinced were natural curls, and even from this distance he could see that her eyes were big and brown. Fawn eyes. Pretty, pretty eyes. She was wearing a simple pale pink sundress that suited her to perfection.

Whew, Luke thought. He'd felt it, a funny little hitch in the much-needed breath he'd taken and the increased tempo of his heart. Nothing like this had ever happened to him before. Nothing. This woman had definitely made a strange and totally unfamiliar impact on him.

Luke continued to watch as the woman attached a mint-green bow to the second pew, then matching ones on the other side of the aisle, making it subtly clear that those four rows were reserved for the families of the bride and groom.

She might, he guessed, be the wedding coordinator whom Ginger had driven to the brink of insanity. She appeared very young for such a lofty title, was maybe twenty-four or twenty-five. So, okay, at thirty-two he wasn't too old for her. Good. That was good.

But…a wedding coordinator? Why did a person decide to become one of those? Because their own wedding had been so wonderful they wanted to share the bliss of an error-free event with others? No. No way. She was not married. That was not acceptable. She was a wedding coordinator because she was a romantic, old-fashioned woman who adored weddings and was very good at taking care of a zillion details at the same time. Yes. That was much better.

He had to meet this woman, Luke thought with a sense of urgency. He had to hear her voice, look deep into those incredible brown eyes of hers. He had to connect with her before she disappeared from his life as quickly as she'd appeared. He had to… Man, he had to get a grip. He didn't know what was happening to him, but it was a tad scary, that was for sure.

The sound of voices on the porch reached Luke and he got to his feet and stepped into the aisle just as the woman turned toward him. She gasped in shock that he was standing there and took a step backward.

"I'm sorry," he said, walking forward. "I didn't mean to startle you. I arrived early and I was just sitting here quietly and…" He stopped in front of her, gazed into her eyes and totally forgot what he was going to say.

"I…" the woman said, still looking directly into his eyes. "I'm…" Whoever I am. Heavens, those eyes, those eyes were dark, fathomless pools that a woman could just drown in and not even struggle to escape. And that voice. So masculine and rumbly and yet…it seemed to stroke her like soft, sensuous velvet, causing her skin to tingle and…

He was tall, had wide shoulders, long legs, rough-hewn features and thick, glorious black hair. He looked like someone straight out of central casting.

"You're…who?" Luke said, leaning slightly toward her.

"Who what?" she said, then blinked. "Oh! Yes, of course. I'm Maggie Jenkins, the wedding coordinator. I own Roses and Wishes, which is gaining a fine reputation for coordinating weddings, because that's what I do. I…coordinate…weddings. I'm also babbling, so forget all that. I'm a tad exhausted at the moment, you see. And you are?"

Enchanted, Luke thought, smiling. Maggie Jenkins. Maggie. He liked her name. It suited her, it really did. Oh, yes, hello, Maggie Jenkins, who was not wearing a wedding ring, thank goodness.

"Luke St. John," he said. "The brother of the nervous groom and the best man for this gala event."

"Pleased to meet you," Maggie said, tearing her gaze

from Luke's. "I believe the others have arrived. I'd better go greet everyone and get this rehearsal going so we stay on schedule, because dinner's booked at the restaurant afterward. Excuse me."

Luke turned to watch her hurry down the aisle as the large group of people appeared. He didn't move to join the others. Not yet. He just stood there drinking in the sight of Maggie.

Maggie stifled a yawn of fatigue as she plastered a plastic smile on her tired face and stopped in front of the chattering wedding party.

Was that heat she felt on her back? she thought suddenly. Was Luke St. John staring at her with those…those eyes? Maggie, stop it. She had made a complete idiot of herself with Luke, had overreacted to his masculine magnetism only because she was so tired she couldn't think straight. Once rested, she would view Luke St. John as a very handsome man but big macho deal.

"Hello, everyone," Maggie said brightly.

"Oh, Maggie," Ginger said, beaming, "isn't this exciting? Tomorrow is the big day. I can hardly believe it's finally here."

You're not the only one, Maggie thought, smiling and nodding at the petite blonde who boasted a golden tan and was wearing a royal-blue raw silk jumpsuit.

"Did I check with you to see if you'd found someone to supply only pale yellow and mint-green yogurt-covered almonds for the nut cups at the reception?" Ginger said, frowning.

"Yes, you did," Maggie said. "And, yes, I did. Well,

sort of. I had to order extra nuts, then pick out the two colors we needed." Which took until after two o'clock this morning. "I was going to ask you what you wanted me to do with the almonds we didn't use."

"Whatever," Ginger said, waving one hand in the air. "Where's my sweetie? Oh, Robert, there you are, honey. Do you realize we'll soon be winging our way to Greece? We'll have a whole month to—What's wrong? You don't look like a happy groom."

The handsome young man in his midtwenties, who was wearing slacks and a dress shirt open at the neck, slid one arm across Ginger's shoulders.

"My brother isn't here yet," he said. "We can't have a rehearsal without the best man."

"I'm right here," Luke said, striding toward the group.

"I'm going to go tell Reverend Mason we're ready to begin the rehearsal," Maggie said quickly. "He's in his office and told me to come get him when we were all set."

"Maggie, hon, wait a sec," an attractive young woman said. "I've lost two pounds since the final fitting of my bridesmaid dress. Do you think it could be nipped in a bit before the ceremony tomorrow night?"

Over my dead body, Maggie thought. Don't even think about it…*hon.*

"That won't be necessary…Tiffy, isn't it?" Maggie said, her voice dripping with sweetness. "That's the beauty of that style of gown. There's room for a fluctuation of a few pounds here and there. I promise that you have nothing to worry about."

Nicely done, Luke thought, swallowing a burst of laughter. Maggie had handled the spoiled and pampered Tiffy like a pro. She was really something, this Maggie Jenkins.

"Look on the bright side, Tiffy," one of the other bridesmaids said. "You can eat your little heart out at the wedding reception—and at the rehearsal dinner tonight, for that matter. You know Ginger and Mrs. Barrington picked goodies to die for. Eat and enjoy."

"Well, there is that, Melissa Ann," Tiffy said thoughtfully, then wandered away.

Bless you, Melissa Ann, Maggie thought wearily.

"And don't forget all those delicious green and yellow yogurt-covered almonds," Luke said, finally indulging in a chuckle. He paused. "Maggie, did you really have to sort through tons of those things to get the two colors?"

"No detail is too small for Roses and Wishes," Maggie said, not looking in Luke's direction.

As Maggie rushed away to get the priest, Luke turned to watch her go, a smile tugging at the corners of his mouth.

"Luke?" Robert said.

"Hmm?" he said, still staring after Maggie.

"What's the matter with you?" Robert said. "You're standing here with your back to everyone. Could you be a little more sociable, for Pete's sake?"

Luke snapped his head around to look at his brother. "Yes, certainly. Sorry." He paused. "I must say, Robert, that I'm impressed with the job Maggie Jenkins has done for you and Ginger. Maggie is quite young to have her own business. It's interesting, too, that she's a wedding coordinator who isn't married." Didn't hurt to double-check on that. "Don't you think? You know, someone who didn't have a fabulous wedding of their own?"

Robert shrugged.

"I asked Maggie about that," Ginger said, joining the brothers and slipping her arm through Robert's. "She pointed out that not all pediatricians have children. Maggie loves the challenge of planning a perfect wedding down to the smallest detail. She just doesn't want one of her own. She told me that. She never intends to get married."

Luke frowned. "Why not?"

"Well, gracious, Luke," Ginger said, wrinkling her nose, "it wouldn't have been polite to ask that. I swear, men should be required to take the same social-graces classes that all of us women do." She shifted her attention to Robert. "Sweetie, what if people don't like yogurt-covered almonds? Do you think I should ask Maggie to change what's in the nut cups before tomorrow night?"

"No," Luke said quickly. "Did you notice the shadows under Maggie's eyes, Ginger? She's obviously exhausted, and I'm sure you learned in your social-graces classes that you should be aware of the needs of those around you.

"Besides, I've attended more gala events than you due to the simple fact that I'm older than you are. I assure you that my vast experience has shown me that most people are very fond of yogurt-covered almonds."

"Really?" Ginger said, beaming.

"Guaranteed," Luke said. "So don't even entertain the idea of asking Maggie to stay up all night redoing the nut cups."

"Well, if you say so, Luke," Ginger said. "I won't… Oh, there's Maggie with Reverend Mason. I'd best go say hi."

Ginger hustled up the aisle and Robert stared at his older brother.

"You're suddenly an expert on the popularity of almonds?" Robert said incredulously. "Where did that come from? And you're aware that Maggie is exhausted? What did she do? Say, 'Hi, I'm Maggie and I'm wiped out'?"

"I'm an attorney, Robert," Luke said. "A good lawyer learns to observe people for subtle little nuances that can be extremely important in the outcome of a given case."

"That is such a bunch of crock," Robert said with a hoot of laughter.

"Yeah, well…" Luke frowned. "Forget it."

"You sure sound—what word do I want?—protective. Yes, that's it, protective of Ms. Maggie, big brother. What gives?"

"Nothing 'gives.' Look, just concentrate on marrying Ginger." Luke paused. "You know, Robert, I'm rather…envious of what you and Ginger have together. I've watched you two over the past months, seen you fall deeply in love, make plans for a future together. It's good and I'm really happy for you both. Yep, I admit I'm a little bit jealous."

"You? Envious of me?" Robert said, splaying one hand on his chest. "I find that a tad hard to believe. You have women beating down your door. You've always gone for the type who just wants to have fun but not settle down. There are seven bridesmaids over there who fit that bill. Just take your pick."

Luke watched Maggie approach with the priest and Ginger.

"Things change," he said quietly.

Reverend Mason greeted everyone and explained that they would walk through the basics of the wedding ceremony so everything would go smoothly the next evening.

"Right," he said finally. "Ginger, if you'll stand at the back of the church with your father and be ready to come down the aisle after your bridesmaids and…"

"Oh, no," Ginger said, shaking her head. "No, no, no, I can't do that."

"Why not?" Robert said frantically. "You're not changing your mind about marrying me, are you?"

"Don't be silly, sweetie," Ginger said, kissing him on the cheek. "But you know how it's bad luck for the groom to see the bride on their wedding day before the ceremony? Well, it's also bad luck for the bride and groom to act out those roles at the rehearsal. Didn't you know that?"

"Can't say that I did," Robert said, drawing a deep breath of relief. "So now what?"

"You and I will sit and watch very carefully," Ginger continued, "so we'll know what we're to do tomorrow night."

"Watch who?" Robert said. "We're the bride and groom, remember?"

"We use stand-ins for the rehearsal, silly," Ginger said. "Let's see. Okay. Your father will be the best man and pretend he has the ring, and Luke will be the groom. And…" She glanced around. "Yes, of course. Maggie, you'll be the bride."

"Got it," Luke said.

"I don't think that's a great idea," Maggie said, feeling the color drain from her face. "No. Bad plan. Bad, bad. I need to… Yes, I need to stay at the back of the church and control the spacing of the bridesmaids starting down the aisle."

"What is the spacing?" Luke said pleasantly.

"Three pews apart, but…"

"Have you got that, ladies?" Luke said, looking at Ginger's girlfriends.

Seven heads bobbed up and down.

"Done," Luke said. "That leaves you free to be way behind them with Ginger's dad ready to be…the bride, Maggie. And I'll be the groom."

"Excellent," Reverend Mason said. "Let's take our places, please. The groomsmen need to be up front with our stand-in best man and groom. Mothers, take your places, please. Ginger and Robert, sit where you can observe and hear me clearly."

"But—" Maggie pointed one finger in the air.

"See you soon, future wife," Luke said, smiling at Maggie.

"But—"

"Come along…Ginger," Mr. Barrington said, chuckling as he tucked Maggie's hand in the crook of his arm. "This reminds me of a baseball game. Instead of a designated hitter, you're the designated bride."

She didn't want to be a bride, Maggie thought miserably as Ginger's father led her to the back of the church. Well, she did, but it would never happen. She wouldn't allow it to happen because… No, she was not a bride. Not a real one or a pretend one or a designated one. Not a bride. Not now, not ever.

And to make matters even worse, the stand-in groom was Luke St. John, a man who had made her forget her own name. Good grief, she wanted to go home. Right now.

Everyone except Maggie was chattering and laughing as they took their places, then silence fell as Reverend Mason raised one hand for quiet. He stood at the front of the church with Luke next to him, then the other men in a straight row alongside.

"The organ music you picked for the procession has now begun," the priest said, smiling. "Pretend you hear it. We're ready for the bridesmaids to come forward. What was it? Oh, yes, three pews apart, my dears."

As Tiffy started off, Ginger's father bent down to whisper to Maggie.

"I hope Ginger looks happier tomorrow night than you do at the moment," he said. "I think this is rather fun, don't you, Maggie?"

"That's not quite the word I would pick, sir," she said, attempting and failing to produce a smile.

"But your groom is Luke St. John," Mr. Barrington

said. "He's considered quite a catch in this town. You have to get into your role and realize you're the envy of a multitude of women in Phoenix. Will that thought make you smile?"

"Not really," Maggie said gloomily.

"Well, fake it. My daughter is so superstitious about all this nonsense that she'll probably pitch a fit if you look like you're about to have a root canal. You can be Ginger marrying Robert or Maggie marrying Luke. Take your pick, but remember this is a wedding, not a funeral. *Smile.*"

Maggie nodded jerkily and plastered such a wide smile on her face that her cheeks hurt.

"Now you look like someone just stepped on your foot," Mr. Barrington said.

"Don't get picky," Maggie said, glaring at him while keeping her plastic smile in place. "This is the best I can do."

"For a wedding coordinator," Mr. Barrington said, "you have a strange attitude about being a bride. Fascinating."

No, try terrifying, Maggie thought. Try never going to happen. Try…*she wanted to go home.*

"Now the actual wedding march begins," Reverend Mason said in the distance. "Give the congregation time to rise and turn in your direction and…now…here comes the lovely bride."

Two

He could hear the wedding march, Luke thought. *He could.* A part of him knew that was impossible, yet it was there quite clearly, the wondrous music filling the church to overflowing.

And in the distance, walking in measured steps on the arm of Ginger's father, was Maggie, his bride. *His.* She was lovely, just exquisite. His heart was thundering at the mere sight of her as she came closer and closer and…

Maggie and Mr. Barrington stopped in front of the priest.

"I will ask at this point," Reverend Mason said, "who gives this woman in marriage. And you, Mr. Barrington, will reply 'Her mother and I,' then you'll take your daughter's hand and place it in Robert's."

"Her mother and I," Mr. Barrington boomed, then grasped Maggie's hand.

Without realizing he had moved, Luke stepped forward and extended his hand to receive Maggie's. As Mr. Barrington placed Maggie's hand in Luke's, their eyes met and time stopped.

Dear heaven, Maggie thought, unable to tear her gaze from the mesmerizing depths of Luke's eyes. Luke's hand was so strong yet so gentle as it wrapped around hers. And the heat. Good grief, the heat from his hand was traveling up her arm, across her breasts, then swirling and churning throughout her, causing a flush she could feel staining her cheeks.

She had to get her hand back. And she would. In a minute.

And she had to quit, just stop, looking into Luke's eyes. And she would. In a minute.

"We are gathered here," Reverend Mason said, "to unite this man and this woman in holy matrimony."

Yes, Luke thought, that was exactly why they were there. This man, him, and this woman, Maggie, were about to be united in holy matrimony, become husband and wife until death parted them.

He had never in his entire life felt like this. He was consumed with a soothing warmth of peace that was somehow combined with the coiling heat of desire. The chill within him that he now knew had been loneliness was gone, pushed into oblivion, never to return because Maggie was here. He'd waited an eternity for this, for her, to find his soul mate, and she was here at long last. Maggie.

Oh, man, this was nuts, he thought, unable to stop a smile from forming on his lips. He was an attorney who dealt in facts, absolutes, things being either black or white, proven data, and… Yet he had suddenly been flung—there was no other word for it—flung helter-skelter into a strange new world that embraced the romantic notion of love at first sight.

Oh, yeah, this was crazy. And wonderful. And hard to believe, but he did believe it with his entire being—heart, mind, body and soul.

Maggie Jenkins had come, she had seen, she had conquered. By doing nothing more than being, she had stolen his heart for all time, and he didn't want it back. Not ever. He loved her. It was as simple and as complicated as that. It was exciting and terrifying at the same time. It couldn't, shouldn't, be true, but yet it was.

He was in forever love with Maggie.

"After you have lit the single candle from the ones that will be burning next to it," Reverend Mason was saying, "blow out the others and place them back in the holders. The single burning candle will represent your union, becoming one entity."

Yes, Luke thought firmly.

Yes, Maggie thought dreamily. Wasn't that just the sweetest thing?

Reverend Mason's word became a buzz, like a multitude of bees in the background, as Maggie and Luke continued to look directly into each other's eyes. Then suddenly what the priest said was loud and clear.

"You may kiss the bride."

Luke framed Maggie's face in his hands, looked at her intently for a long, heart-stopping moment, then slowly, so slowly, lowered his head and captured her lips in a kiss that was so tender, so reverent, so…theirs, that tears filled Maggie's eyes. She savored the taste, the feel, the very essence of Luke, yearning for the kiss to never end.

Reverend Mason cleared his throat. "Yes, well, that's fine. Thank you, Luke, Maggie, for playing out your roles so convincingly."

Luke raised his head and both he and Maggie stared at the priest as though they had never seen him before in their lives.

"I, um…" Reverend Mason continued, "I will then introduce Mr. and Mrs. Robert St. John to the congregation, the organ music will burst forth and the recessional will take place. Any questions?"

Ginger jumped to her feet. "No, no questions. It's going to be so beautiful. I can hardly wait until tomorrow night. Thank you so much, Reverend Mason. We're off to the restaurant now for the rehearsal dinner. I do hope you and your wife will join us as planned."

"We'd be delighted," he said, sliding one more glance at Luke and Maggie, who were still staring at him with rather stunned expressions on their faces.

Maggie shook her head slightly to escape from the eerie spell that seemed to have transported her to a faraway place. She stepped back from Luke, averting her eyes, then spun around and forced another big smile onto her lips. Lips that still held the taste of Luke, the feel of Luke, tingled from the kiss shared with Luke.

"Ginger," Maggie said, "I'll come to the restaurant to make certain that everything is as it should be, then I'm going to scoot on home."

"But you're supposed to have dinner with us, Maggie," Ginger said, pouting prettily.

"I had a late lunch," Maggie said. "I couldn't eat a bite. Really."

"Don't be silly, my dear," Mr. Barrington said. "We all know how hard you've worked all these months to make this event perfect for our Ginger. I insist that you join us for dinner, even if you don't eat much. Good. That's settled. Me? I'm starving. Let's get going."

"But—" Maggie said.

"Come along, Mrs. St. John," Luke said, encircling her shoulders with his arm.

"What?" Maggie said, staring up at him with wide eyes. "Who?"

"Oh, sorry," Luke said, smiling. "I'm still in my role, I guess. You and I did get married a few minutes ago, you know. Maggie St. John. It has a nice ring to it, don't you think?"

"*Ginger* St. John has a nice ring to it," she said. "That's who I was pretending to be, remember? I'm Maggie *Jenkins* and that's who I intend to remain."

"Ah," Luke said, nodding.

"And what does 'ah' mean?" she said.

"Only that none of us have crystal balls to see into the future, Maggie *Jenkins*," he said. "Who knows what might happen? Shall we go?"

Without speaking further, Maggie grabbed the box

that had held the satin bows, then marched down the aisle, snatching her purse from the last pew as she went.

Outside the summer sky was a black velvet canopy sprinkled with twinkling diamondlike stars and a silvery moon, all of which went unnoticed by Maggie as she stomped to her ten-year-old van and slid behind the wheel.

As she took her place in the line of vehicles headed to the restaurant she drew a deep, shuddering breath.

Don't think, she ordered herself. Don't dwell on what took place in that church. Don't relive that kiss, or see again the smoldering passion in Luke's eyes or feel the tenderness of his hands on her flushed face or acknowledge the desire that had swept through her. Do not do that, Maggie Jenkins. Okay. Fine. She wouldn't. *She would not.*

But, darn it, what had happened back there? She had never in her life experienced anything so…so…whatever that had been. It was as though everyone had disappeared, leaving only her and Luke in a wondrous place that was theirs alone. The bride. The groom. The kiss. The undefinable something that in its intensity took desire beyond description. Luke.

Maggie sighed. It was a dreamy, wistful, womanly sigh that caused a soft smile to form on her lips. In the next instant she smacked the steering wheel with the palm of her hand.

"Cut it out, Maggie Jenkins," she yelled. "Just stop it right now. You are acting so ridiculous, it's a crime."

It was amazing, she mentally rushed on, how asinine a person could behave, think, feel, when they were totally exhausted. That, of course, was the explanation for what had happened. Overreaction due to overfatigue. It was all so simple now that she calmed down and thought about it like a rational human being.

At least no one had been aware of how silly she'd behaved while performing in her role of the bride. Well, Reverend Mason had given her and Luke a rather inquisitive look, but everyone else had been oblivious to the nonsense between them.

Well, that was probably not even accurate. Luke had been doing a stand-in thing for his brother, nothing more. She was the one who had gotten all wiggy and weird, not him. Luke had just been pretending to be Robert and seeing her as Ginger. End of story.

Maggie flicked on her blinker and followed the cars into the parking lot of the restaurant.

She'd nibble a bit of dinner, she thought, then be on her way home to bed as quickly as was socially acceptable. Everything was fine. Just fine. She was erasing what had happened from her beleaguered mind. So there.

As the chattering group entered the restaurant, Robert pulled Luke to one side and spoke to his older brother in a quiet voice.

"Luke, my man," Robert said, "care to explain what was going on between you and Maggie during that rehearsal?"

"What do you mean?" Luke said. "We were just playing out the roles Ginger assigned us, that's all."

"Yeah, right," Robert said with a snort. "From where I was sitting, it didn't look like 'let's pretend.' No way.

You've been acting very strange ever since you met Maggie, Luke."

"Robert, Robert, Robert," Luke said, shaking his head. "You've got a typical case of prewedding jitters, not thinking clearly, seeing things that aren't there, the whole nine yards. You'd better get it together or you're liable to pass out at the altar tomorrow night. Trust me. I've been in a great many wedding parties over the years and I've seen your symptoms time and again."

"Really?" Robert said, pressing a fingertip on his chest. "Now that you mention it, my heart is beating really fast."

"That's one of the signs," Luke said, nodding. "I'm telling you, little brother, you've got to calm down. Ginger will never forgive you if you spoil this shindig by falling flat on your face before you can say 'I do.'"

"You're right," Robert said. "Okay. Deep breath. In. Out. I'm cool. I'm fine."

"Robert," Ginger said, coming back to where the brothers were standing. "They're waiting to seat us. Is something wrong?"

"Robert was just very emotionally moved by the rehearsal at the church," Luke said. "But all is well now. You're marrying a very romantic man here, Ginger."

"Ohhh, you are so sweet," Ginger said, giving Robert a quick kiss on the lips. "I love you so much."

"I love you, too, sugar," Robert said.

And unbelievable as it was, Luke thought, he loved Maggie Jenkins. This was definitely a fantastic life-changing night.

The restaurant where the dinner was being held was a five-star establishment, and Maggie had reserved a private dining room for the wedding party.

"Oh," she said softly when she entered the room.

Everything looked wonderful. The staff had really gone all out, per her instructions. The chandeliers were dimmed to create a rosy hue over the room. The crystal glasses gleamed and the sterling silverware sparkled. Wafer-thin china finger bowls sat by each place setting, and yellow rose petals were scattered whimsically down the center of the table that was covered in a pristine white cloth with lace edging.

Nodding in approval at the lovely and oh-so-romantic atmosphere, Maggie hung back with the intention of claiming a seat close to the door so she could make her early exit without creating a fuss. Just as she was about to sit down, Luke took her arm.

"Whoa," he said. "The pretend bride and groom are supposed to sit close to the real bride and groom at this dinner. It's part of the superstition."

"It is not," Maggie said, frowning.

"It certainly is," Luke said indignantly. "You wouldn't want to upset Ginger, would you? I mean, hey, anyone who spends hours sorting through yogurt-covered almonds to get the proper colors for the nut cups certainly wouldn't do anything to blow it in the home stretch."

"Well, Roses and Wishes does aim to please."

"My point exactly," Luke said, propelling Maggie toward the middle of the table. "Which is why you and I are going to sit close to the bride and groom before Ginger flips out."

"But I don't intend to stay long and I—"

"Here we are," Luke said, pulling out a chair. "Right across from the happy couple."

"Mmm," Maggie said, shooting a glare in Luke's direction, then plunking down in the chair.

Waitresses appeared, wineglasses were filled. Soups, then salads came and went. Then huge plates of roast beef, baked potatoes and artfully arranged asparagus were set in front of the diners.

Maggie stifled yet another yawn and stared down at the meal.

"Eat," Luke whispered in her ear.

"I'm too tired to eat."

"If you don't eat, Ginger will think something has gone wrong with the wedding plans and you're upset," Luke said, "which will cause her to—" he shuddered "—I don't even want to think about it."

Maggie sighed and picked up her fork.

The conversations around the table were lively with laughter erupting from one end of the table, then later the other. Everyone was having a wonderful time.

And Maggie was falling asleep.

The four sips of wine she'd consumed were her final undoing, and she was suddenly unable to keep her eyes open. Just as she began to slide off the front of her chair, Luke flung his arm around her and hauled her back up. Maggie blinked and shook her head slightly.

"That was a great story, Maggie," Luke said, his arm

still holding her upright. "Really funny. Ah, here comes the waitress with some coffee. Would you care for some? Yes, you would."

"Yes, I would," Maggie mumbled.

"I want to hear the funny story," Ginger said. "Share with us, Maggie."

"Um…" Maggie said, a blank expression on her face.

"Right," Luke said. "Well, you see, Maggie coordinated a wedding where the bride and groom wanted to be married on horseback. That included the minister sitting on a huge stallion, you understand. The stallion was a horny beast, and just as the minister was to pronounce the couple officially wed, the stallion caught the scent of a mare in an adjoining pasture and took off—bam!— just whisked that minister away in a trail of dust."

Everyone erupted in appropriate laughter, then continued on with their own conversations.

"That was the dumbest thing I've ever heard," Maggie said to Luke under her breath.

"I thought it was pretty good considering I was winging it," Luke said, smiling at her.

"Would you please remove your arm from my person before someone wonders why it is there?"

"Just as soon as you get a few jolts of caffeine in you, my bride," Luke said.

"I am not your bride," Maggie said through clenched teeth. "Your arm is disturbing me."

"Oh?"

"What I mean is," she said, "it's heavy. Your arm. And warm. Much too warm. The air-conditioning is on, but there are a great many people in this room and...much too warm. Hot."

"You're hot?" Luke said, an expression of pure innocence on his face. "Because I have my arm around you? Because I'm very close to you and you're very close to me? Isn't that interesting?"

The waitress filled Maggie's coffee cup, then Luke's, then moved on down the table. Maggie leaned forward to grasp her cup, aware that Luke's arm seemed to be permanently attached to her body. She took a sip of coffee, blew on the remainder to cool it, then drained the cup.

"All better," she said. "I'm wide awake, ready to rock and roll. You may have your arm back now, Luke." That strong, masculine and oh-so-hot arm. "Thank you for your assistance."

"Glad to help," Luke said slowly, very slowly removing his arm. He paused. "So tell me, Maggie, why is it that someone whose focus is on producing picture-perfect weddings doesn't want a wedding of her own? Someone mentioned that you don't intend to marry. I'm curious as to why."

"It's a long story," Maggie said, running one fingertip around the rim of her coffee cup.

"I'm listening."

"I'd rather not discuss it." Maggie pushed her chair back and got to her feet. "Thank you for a lovely dinner," she said to Ginger and Robert. "I'll see everyone at the church tomorrow night. 'Bye for now."

"Hey, wait a minute," Luke said, getting quickly to

his feet. "I think it would be best if I drove you home. You might fall asleep at the wheel."

"Oh, no, I'm perfectly fine now that I've had that coffee. Ta ta."

As Maggie hurried from the room with a chorus of goodbyes following her out the door, Luke slouched back in his chair, a frown knitting his brows.

"Damn coffee," he said, looking at Maggie's empty cup.

"What's wrong with the coffee?" Ginger said, peering into her own cup.

"It's fine, honey," Robert said, then slid a grin at Luke. "It perks up sleepy people that other people wish hadn't gotten perked."

"Pardon me?" Ginger said.

"Nothing," Robert said, chuckling. "It's a guy thing between me and Luke. You know Luke, Ginger. He was the groom tonight and Maggie was the bride. Don't you think they made a smashing couple?"

"We're going to discuss smashing in regard to your nose if you don't shut up," Luke said.

Robert burst into laughter. Ginger looked totally confused. Mrs. St. John told her sons to behave themselves, and Luke got to his feet and said he was leaving.

"Great meal," he said. "In fact, the entire evening was very special. Definitely memorable."

"Do tell," Robert said, still beaming.

Luke made an imaginary gun out of his thumb and forefinger and shot his brother, who laughed so hard he got the hiccups.

* * *

Roses and Wishes took up the first floor of an older Victorian house that Maggie rented in an area of Phoenix that had been rezoned for businesses. Maggie lived upstairs, having furnished one of the bedrooms as a small living room.

The kitchen was on the main floor, as well as a powder room. The original living room was the reception area where albums with pictures of weddings were displayed and comfortable chairs grouped for discussing forthcoming ceremonies. The dining room was Maggie's office.

Maggie's favorite feature of the entire place was the enormous old-fashioned claw-foot bathtub in the upstairs bathroom that allowed her to indulge in long, leisurely soaks with soothing warm water up to her chin.

An hour after leaving the restaurant, having battled the traffic to get home, Maggie sank gratefully into the beckoning bubbles in the tub, rested her head on a spongy pillow on the rim and closed her eyes.

Good grief, she thought, what a night this had been. It had been awful, just awful. Luke St. John was a menace. Yes, that was a great word. A menace. A very dangerous, sensuous member of the male species who was a…a menace to her state of mind and did funny little weird things to her body. Her libido or some such thing. Her womanliness in general. He had nudged awake desire within her that she had worked very hard to put to sleep, to tuck away and ignore. Definitely a menace.

No wonder he had women crawling out of the woodwork trying to get his attention. He had an unexplainable something that pushed sexual buttons in women that they didn't even know they possessed.

Well, she was wise to him now. Granted, part of her overreaction to Luke St. John was due to her exhaustion, but she had a sneaky feeling that even well-rested she might be susceptible to his whatever-it-was.

So. Tomorrow night at the wedding and the reception following she was going to make very certain that she kept her distance from Mr. St. John.

There would be no more gazing into his incredible eyes. No more strong, *hot* arms encircling her. And heaven forbid, no more kisses shared that caused her to have naughty images of tearing his clothes off and ravishing his body right there in front of Reverend Mason.

There. It was settled. She had her plan. She'd stay away from Luke tomorrow night, the wedding would take place without a hitch and she'd never see him again.

Maggie opened her eyes and frowned.

Never see Luke again? Never? Ever? No, of course she wouldn't. He was a member of the jet-set money crowd, and she was among those who hoped they could make next month's rent. There was simply no way that their paths would cross again.

Why was that depressing?

"Oh, stop it," she said aloud, then closed her eyes again.

That was a thought from the tired part of her brain that the coffee hadn't reached. She was now blanking her mind, relaxing in her wonderful bathtub, preparing to sleep away the hours of the night and awake rejuvenated and back to normal with no lingering images or wanton thoughts of Luke St. John.

"Mmm," Maggie said, feeling the misty fog of sleep begin to dim her senses. "Mmm."

Maggie began to slide slowly lower in the tub. Then lower and lower…until she disappeared beneath the frothy bubbles.

She shot upward, sputtering as she swallowed a mouthful of suds, the wild motions causing water to splash out of the tub and onto the floor.

Her hair was covered in bubbles, which made her look like a frosted cake and, she knew, would result in a sticky mess that would have to be properly shampooed. The floor would have to be mopped, her towel that she'd placed next to the tub was soaked and…

And Maggie burst into tears.

She cried because she'd scared herself to death by sinking under the water and because the bubbles tasted terrible and now her stomach was upset. She cried because she was too tired to shampoo her hair and mop the floor and deal with a soggy towel and…

She cried because no matter how hard she tried she couldn't forget what it had been like to be kissed by Luke St. John and she didn't know how to deal with all the new and foreign feelings she'd experienced.

She cried because after tomorrow night she'd never see Luke again, which *she knew,* she knew, was for the best, but sometimes the best was really stinky and just so sad.

She cried because…because, darn it anyway, she felt like it.

So Maggie cried until she had no more tears to shed and the water in the tub was cold and her hair had dried and was a gummy disaster sticking up in weird spiky things and her sinuses were clogged, causing a roaring headache.

Maggie sniffled as she got out of the tub, picked up the soggy towel and threw it in the water. She marched into her bedroom and crawled beneath the sheets.

And during the night spent on damp linens and a gooey pillow, she dreamed of Luke St. John.

Three

Unable to sleep after the events of the unsettling evening, Luke gave up and left his bed, pulling on a lightweight robe. He wandered through his penthouse apartment, finally stopping by a wall of windows to look out over the city lights that shone into infinity.

Thoughts tumbled through his mind one after another, and he pressed the heels of his hands to his throbbing temples for a moment in a futile attempt to halt the onslaught.

Maggie, he thought, crossing his arms over his chest. She was all and everything he had ever hoped to find in a woman. He had only known her for a handful of hours, yet he knew she was the one, his life's partner.

Half of him wanted to shout the fantastic news from

the rooftops, tell the world that he was in love, had found the woman of his heart.

Another section of his being was terrified that Maggie would never come to feel the same way about him, that she would slip away from him like sand falling from the palm of his hand.

Maggie, for reasons she refused to share so far, never intended to marry. That was not good, not good at all. The mystifying question was why. Had she been terribly hurt by a man in the past? Oh, he'd take the guy apart. He'd…Whoa, he would just waste mental energy going off in that direction.

Maybe Maggie was so focused on her career she saw no room for a man in her life. No, that didn't work for him. He'd dated a multitude of women with that mindset and they were all popped out of the same mold. Maggie wasn't like them, not even close. She didn't have the brittle edginess, that step-over-the-bodies-to-get-to-the-top mentality he was so tired of dealing with.

Maggie was so down to earth, so…real. She'd started a business that made dreams come true for brides, made their weddings a special, memory-making event in their lives.

Ginger and Robert's day was going to be perfect because Maggie had seen to every detail, including sorting through a mountain of yogurt-covered almonds to select Ginger's choice of colors.

Yes, Maggie knew how to make dreams come true, yet she didn't want any of those spectacular weddings to be hers, didn't want to be the bride who would see her groom waiting eagerly for her at the altar as she made her way down the aisle.

Why?

It was as though Maggie had built tall, strong walls around her heart, and his greatest fear was that he wouldn't be able to break through them, get a chance to capture her heart as she had his.

The flicker of hope he had, Luke mused as he continued to stare out the window, was that he'd felt Maggie respond to his kiss during the rehearsal, had seen the desire in her big brown eyes directed toward him. *Him.*

That kiss had been the beginning of the chipping away of that barrier surrounding Maggie. It was a start, a positive one, but he had a long, long way to go.

His first impulse was to ask Maggie out, wine and dine and court her, but a cold knot in his gut told him she'd turn him down flat if he invited her to join him for a night on the town. She'd been upset, really flustered by her reaction to the kiss they'd shared and had beat a hasty retreat from the rehearsal dinner as quickly as she could.

No, the traditional program of flowers, candy and romantic dinners wasn't going to work because he just somehow knew he wasn't going to get a chance to put those things in motion.

He needed a new and innovative plan, Luke thought, narrowing his eyes. And he'd better come up with it very quickly. He'd see Maggie at the wedding and reception, but beyond that he envisioned her being set on automatic "no" if he attempted to get her to go out with him.

Ah, Maggie, why? he thought dismally. What secret

something held her in an iron fist that made her determined to never fall in love, never marry, never be the bride in one of her meticulously planned weddings?

He didn't know the answer to that tormenting question. Nor did he know the answer to how he was going to see Maggie again after Robert and Ginger's wedding. And he didn't know the answer to how he would face a cold and empty future without her.

Well, the first order of business, he thought, heading back toward his bedroom, was to get some sleep. He was about to begin the greatest battle of his life and he intended to win. Somehow. He would be the victor. Somehow. He would crumble Maggie's walls into dust and share her sunshine world with her for all time. Somehow.

Late the next morning Maggie entered the small house where her mother lived and presented her with a lumpy plastic bag.

"What's this, sweetheart?" Martha Jenkins said, holding the bag at eye level.

"Almonds," Maggie said, sitting down at the kitchen table. "Yogurt-covered almonds in every shade of the rainbow except yellow and mint-green."

Martha laughed as she sat opposite Maggie and opened the bag. Martha was a rather attractive woman, although not one that would turn heads when she walked into a room. Her brown hair was streaked with gray, which she felt no need to hide, and she had given up long ago trying to lose the twenty pounds that had crept up on her over the years.

"Just what my pudgy person doesn't need," she said. "But, what the heck, I'll eat every one of them. Are these left over from something you did for the big wedding tonight?" She popped two of the nuts into her mouth.

Maggie nodded. "Nut cups. Nut cups, you understand, that only boast yellow and mint-green yogurt-covered almonds, to please my picky bride." She paused. "No, that's not fair. Ginger is very sweet. She just had trouble making up her mind about things for a stretch of time there. But when you think about it, she has every right to have things perfect for her special event."

"That's true," Martha said, then sighed. "But that doesn't guarantee a happy marriage, does it? The bubble bursts and that's that, as evidenced by the fact that I divorced your father when you were ten. Off he went, never to be seen or heard from again." She ate four more almonds. "These are yummy."

"I think Ginger and Robert are going to be a forever couple, Mom," Maggie said. "If you could see them together… Oh, never mind."

"Maggie, honey, I worry so about you," Martha said. "Why on earth did you become a wedding coordinator when there are so many other things you could have done? Why torture yourself creating those beautiful events for other people when—"

"When I know I can never get married myself?" Maggie finished for her.

"Yes," Martha said, patting her daughter's hand. "Exactly."

A sudden and vivid image of Luke flashed through Maggie's mind and a shiver coursed through her.

"Maybe you're right," she said quietly. "Maybe launching Roses and Wishes was a terrible mistake. I've been fine for the past year with all the preparations being for other people, but…" She stopped and shook her head.

"Is there something different about this wedding that's upsetting you?" Martha said, frowning.

"No, not really," Maggie said quickly, forcing a smile to appear on her lips. "It's just the largest wedding I've done, and after so many months I think I'm just registering a sense of loss, sort of hating to say goodbye to all those people.

"I'm hoping, of course, that my reputation will soar because of Ginger and Robert's event and I'll get to do some ritzier weddings. I guess that's what I want. Oh, ignore me. I'm in a strange mood. Eat another almond, Mom. Yogurt is good for a person."

"Nuts are fattening," Martha said, laughing.

"How are things at the store?"

"Same old, same old," Martha said with a shrug. "I manage the children's clothing department by rote now, I've been doing it for so long. I don't love it, I don't hate it, I just do it. Keeps this roof over my head. I really can't complain, sweetheart. I made my way up the ladder from a salesclerk to the manager and I'm proud of that."

"You should be," Maggie said, nodding. "I'm proud of you, too."

"I'll just keep plugging along until I retire. Since I

just turned fifty, I have a ways to go, though." Martha paused. "Do you feel that type of settled in with Roses and Wishes? Do you see yourself running your business for many years to come?"

"I'm not sure," Maggie said, then popped an almond in her mouth. "As I said, I'm having sort of a letdown after working on this big wedding so long. I'll have a better idea how I really feel after tonight and I get some more sleep, sleep, sleep. I'm exhausted and now isn't the time to analyze how I feel about Roses and Wishes."

"True." Martha nodded, then sighed. "Oh, Maggie, I wish things were different. I'd like to think you'd be planning one of those beautiful weddings for yourself someday, but... Hardly seems fair, does it? I know, I know, no one said that life is fair."

"No," Maggie said quietly, "no one said that."

Mother and daughter chatted for a while longer, Martha bringing Maggie up to date on the gossip in the neighborhood, including the news that another of Maggie's childhood friends was getting married, which did nothing to improve Maggie's rather gloomy mood.

Another bride, she thought as she hugged her mother, then left the house. Another bride that wasn't her. Her mom had said she'd reminded the bride-to-be about Roses and Wishes but, due to a very limited budget, the newly engaged couple planned to exchange vows at the courthouse.

No, she thought as she drove away, she wasn't getting more depressed by the minute because her friend hadn't chosen Roses and Wishes to plan her wedding. It was because her friend was *having* a wedding, had found her special someone and would live happily ever after.

Happily ever after, Maggie mused, then sighed. Every bride and groom believed that was their destiny, that they would be together until death parted them, and for some that was gloriously true. But for others?

"Don't go there, Maggie," she ordered herself aloud. "Go home and eat a ton of yogurt-covered almonds and quit thinking." She drew a wobbly breath. "And whatever you do, do *not* dwell on Luke St. John."

Months ago Maggie had splurged on what she referred to in her mind as The Dress. It was sea-green chiffon with a camisole top and a skirt that swirled in changing hues of color just below her knees. Her shoes were strappy evening sandals with three-inch heels. If the event was during the Phoenix winter, she added a lacy off-white shawl that had belonged to her grandmother.

The fact that she wore the same dress to each wedding was immaterial, she knew, because she went unnoticed, was just a busy figure in the background who bustled around making certain everything went as planned.

Wearing The Dress, Maggie arrived at the church an hour before the ceremony was to begin and checked to see that the flowers were delivered and in place. Two of the candles in front of the altar were yellow, and the single one that represented Ginger and Robert united was mint-green.

Maggie stood in the silent church in front of the candles, remembering how Reverend Mason had explained their meaning while she and Luke were playing out the roles of bride and groom.

Knowing she was acting ridiculous, Maggie slid one of the yellow tapers free, then glanced to the right, envisioning Luke holding the other one. In her mind's eye she saw them moving at the same time, igniting the one larger candle in the center. She blew out the imaginary flame that declared her to be a single entity and saw—oh, yes, she really saw—the dancing light from the larger candle in the middle.

Maggie, stop it, she ordered herself as she replaced the yellow taper. Enough of this foolishness.

She turned and her breath caught as she saw Luke standing at the back of the church, watching her as he held a garment bag over his shoulder with one finger.

Squaring her shoulders and lifting her chin, she walked up the aisle to where Luke stood.

"Hello, Luke," she said, looking at an empty space just above his head. "I was just making certain the candles weren't stuck in the holders or anything. Details, details, details. You just wouldn't believe how many little things there are to keep track of for an event like this. And that's my job, by golly, checking all those details and…"

"You look beautiful." Luke's voice was rich, deep and so very male and sensuous that a shiver coursed through Maggie. "Pretty as a bride."

"Oh, well, thank you," Maggie said, still not meeting his gaze. "This is The Dress. What I mean is— Never mind. It's not important. I assume that's your tux you're holding. Ginger changed her mind three times on the color of the tuxedos before settling on pale gray. I hope you don't mind wearing a ruffled shirt, because she didn't budge on ruffled shirts. So. Well. I'd best go into the bride's dressing room and…"

"Maggie, look at me," Luke said quietly.

"Gosh, I just don't have time to do that, Luke."

"Look…at…me."

Maggie slowly shifted her eyes to Luke's and immediately felt light-headed, as though she might float off into oblivion.

"Yes?" she said softly.

"Will you save me a dance at the reception?"

"No, I can't because I don't actually take part, per se, in the reception activities. I hover around in the background checking those pesky little details I told you about. So, nope, no dance. Sorry 'bout that. Gotta go. 'Bye."

"Maggie, do I make you nervous?" Luke said, frowning.

"Nervous? Me?" she said, waving one hand in the air. "Don't be silly. It's not you, it's the whole evening ahead. The reputation of Roses and Wishes is at stake here. Everything has to be perfect."

"Ah," he said, nodding. "That includes keeping all members of the wedding party happy. Right?"

"Well, yes, I suppose so."

"Then promise you'll dance with me. Just one dance, Maggie. That's not too much to ask, is it? You wouldn't want to make the best man grumpy, would you? Heaven forbid."

Maggie narrowed her eyes. "Do you always get what you want, Luke?"

"When it's very important to me, I do," he said, still looking directly into her eyes. "Is it a deal? One dance?"

"Jeez Louise, all right," Maggie said. "But if some detail goes wrong while I'm dancing that dance, it will be your fault, Luke St. John."

"Fair enough," he said, smiling. "I'll see you later then."

"Fine," she said, then scooted around him and hurried away.

Luke stood statue-still for a long moment, staring at the candles that symbolized two becoming one. He nodded, then turned and walked slowly toward the room where the men in the wedding party were to change into their pale gray tuxedos.

Maggie had prepared herself to deal with a totally jangled and nervous-to-the max prewedding Ginger. To Maggie's amazement and heartfelt delight, Ginger had a quiet serenity about her when she arrived in the dressing room at the church.

"Are you really okay?" Maggie said, peering at the bride.

"I'm about to marry the man I love with my whole heart, Maggie," Ginger said softly. "That's all I can think about, focus on. It's strange, isn't it? I made such a fuss about having the right colored almonds in the nut cups, and suddenly none of that is important."

"I think that's wonderful," Maggie said, smiling.

"And you're absolutely beautiful in your dress, Ginger. I hope you and Robert will be very, very happy together."

"Oh, we will be," Ginger said, nodding. "We will be."

Forever? Maggie thought. Until death parted them and even beyond? What were the chances of that?

"Mother," Ginger said, bringing Maggie back to the moment at hand, "you've got to stop crying or you'll be all blotchy in the photographs."

"I know, I know," Mrs. Barrington said, dabbing at her nose with yet another tissue. "But you're my baby girl and… Ohhh, I'm a wreck."

"It's time," Maggie said, looking at her watch. "Mothers, please go and have the ushers seat you now. Bridesmaids, head for the vestibule. You're all simply gorgeous."

"I look like one of those yogurt-covered almonds," Tiffy said, frowning at her reflection in the mirror. "I don't want to do this."

Maggie stepped in front of Tiffy to block her view of herself in the mirror.

"If you want to live to see another day," Maggie said so only Tiffy could hear, "you'll go get in line, Tiffy."

"You can't talk to me like that."

"I just did," Maggie said.

"Oh. Right. Okay. I'm going," Tiffy said, giving Maggie a wary look, then hurrying from the room.

Maggie threw up her hands. "Well, if Tiffy ever gets married, Roses and Wishes sure isn't going to get the chance to coordinate *her* wedding."

* * *

Over three hundred guests witnessed the wedding of Ginger Barrington and Robert St. John. From her usual place in the last pew in the church, Maggie Jenkins indulged herself by watching Luke St. John during the entire picture-perfect ceremony.

What Luke did for a pale gray tuxedo, she thought dreamily, was sinful. The color accentuated his dark hair and tanned skin. The custom-tailored tux made his shoulders look a block wide. And those strong but gentle hands produced the ring right on cue.

The smile that broke across Luke's face when Robert kissed his wife sent shivers coursing down Maggie's spine.

Reverend Mason introduced Mr. and Mrs. Robert St. John to the congregation, then the organ music swelled and the recessional took place, the smiling bride and groom leading the way back down the aisle. When Luke and the maid of honor went by where Maggie stood, he met her gaze for a brief moment and a frisson of heat swirled throughout her.

How on earth, Maggie thought, very aware of her racing heart, was she going to survive her dance with Luke? A promise was a promise, but… If she was just so busy tending to those details, details, details and managed to keep some distance between her and Luke, the dance might never take place. It would take some fancy footwork on her part and she'd have to stay on red alert as to where Luke was at all times, but she could pull this off.

"Good plan," she said under her breath. "Maggie, you're brilliant."

* * *

The reception was being held at one of the exclusive country clubs in Phoenix. A dinner buffet greeted the guests and the huge ballroom was filled with a multitude of round tables each topped with a mint-green or yellow tablecloth and contrasting color candle burning in a glass cylinder in the center. A ten-piece band would play quietly during the meal, then change to Ginger's choice of dance music after the champagne toasts had been made and the four-tier cake had been cut and served by the army of waiters.

As everything continued to go like clockwork, Maggie began to relax and a wave of utter fatigue swept over her. She sat on a folding chair in a dim corner of the room, nibbling on a small plate of food, and nodded in approval at the final outcome of her months of labor.

She'd done it, she thought. Roses and Wishes had hopefully now wiggled its way into the high-society scene of Phoenix. She'd seen the business cards she'd propped next to the candleholder on each table being slipped into purses and given to men to place in their pockets. Fantastic.

Maggie frowned as she recalled the conversation with her mother regarding whether Maggie truly wanted to continue to plan weddings for bride after bride while knowing she herself would never have that title. Well, she wasn't going to dwell on that now, for heaven's sake. She intended to bask in her glory tonight of a job well done for Ginger and Robert St. John.

Maggie placed her plate on the tray of a passing

waiter, then smiled as Ginger and Robert took the floor for the first dance.

How lovely, she thought. They looked so happy, had eyes only for each other as they moved around the gleaming expanse. They danced so well together and—

Maggie suddenly sat bolt upright in her chair.

Dancing, she thought frantically. Other couples were now joining the bride and groom to enjoy the terrific music and so many people were dancing, for heaven's sake. Where was Luke? She had to keep careful track of Luke.

There he was dancing with Ginger. Now he'd shifted to his mother. Fine. My, my, he was poetry in motion, so graceful for a man of his size. Oops. He'd bowed slightly and given his mother's hand to his father and— no, no, no—he was headed toward her secret little corner, was working his way through the crowd on the dance floor. She was out of there.

Maggie jumped to her feet and hurried to the head table, where she gave instructions for the top layer of the cake to be boxed up so it could be frozen and brought out again on Ginger and Robert's first anniversary celebration.

"Give it to the mother of the bride," Maggie told a waiter. "She agreed to take care of it tonight."

"You told us that at the meeting we had last week," the waiter said, frowning. "I've got it covered, Maggie."

"Of course you do," Maggie said, patting him on the arm. "I'm sorry for nagging." She looked quickly into the distance and saw Luke advancing. "How's the supply of champagne holding up?"

"Fine," the waiter said, rolling his eyes. "Trust me. Everything is going great. Isn't there something else you should be doing?"

"Right." Maggie pointed one finger in the air. "I do believe I'll visit the powder room."

"Good idea," the man said drily. "Don't feel you have to check back here."

"Keep up the great work," Maggie said, then rushed away.

When Maggie entered the powder room, she absently registered the fact that it was bigger than her entire living space at home. There was a huge sitting area with love seats, easy chairs and coffee tables holding attractive baskets of artificial flowers.

Beyond all of that were the stalls, a long mirror surrounded by makeup bulbs and a vanity with eight or ten sinks. The noise level was high as women stood two deep in front of the mirror, touching up their postdinner lipstick, one row peering over the shoulders of the other as they chatted and laughed, a good time obviously being had by all.

There was no point in staying in here with this crowd, Maggie thought, shaking her head. The noise was enough to give her a headache and, besides, her purse was locked in a cabinet in the kitchen, so she had nothing to repair her lipstick with.

Well, there was no problem really about leaving the powder room, because even if Luke had figured out where she had been headed, he wouldn't do anything as crass as to plant himself outside the door of the women's restroom. People with money were very big on proper social decorum, and that maneuver definitely wouldn't go down well here.

Nodding in satisfaction that she was so far doing a dandy job of keeping a safe distance between herself and Luke, Maggie opened the door and walked out into the hallway beyond.

And walked smack-dab into the solid, unmoving body of Luke St. John.

Four

Maggie gasped and staggered slightly, causing Luke to grip her upper arms to steady her.

"Well," he said, not releasing his hold on her, "fancy meeting you here, Maggie."

"Luke," she said, looking quickly to each side, "you can't hang around outside the women's restroom. It's not…couth, not nice at all. Your mother would be mortified."

"My mother isn't here," he said, frowning. "You are. Ever since the music began you've been bouncing around the room out there like a Ping-Pong ball. I have the distinct impression that you don't intend to keep your promise to dance with me. Talk about mortifying a mother. How would yours feel if she knew her daughter hadn't kept her word?"

Maggie opened her mouth to say something in her defense, only to realize she was guilty as charged.

"How about," she said, narrowing her eyes in concentration, "I had details, details, details to check on?"

"Nope," Luke said. "Everything is going like a fine-tuned machine. I'm betting that there's nothing left to check on."

"Oh." Maggie paused. "Well, then, try this. I needed to freshen my lipstick, like all the others in the powder room are doing."

"I might buy that," Luke said, nodding, "except where is your tube of lipstick? No purse, no lipstick."

"Oh."

"Maggie," Luke said, his voice gentling, "don't you want to dance with me?"

"Yes, I do. It's just that I—"

"Good. That's settled then." Luke released her arms and grasped one of her hands with one of his. "Let's go."

"But…"

The door to the powder room opened and three young women emerged, stopping before they bumped into Luke and Maggie.

"Well, Luke St. John," one of the women said, smiling coyly, "what on earth are you doing skulking around outside our private little place? Are you lost, gorgeous man?"

"Not at all," Luke said, tightening his hold on Maggie's hand as she tried to pull free. "I just came to collect my partner for the next waltz. I thought it would be extremely polite on my part to escort her to the dance floor."

"Well, isn't that just the sweetest thing?" one of the other women said.

"That's the way I see it," Luke said. "Come along, Maggie."

"You're a lucky girl, Maggie," the third woman said with a wistful sigh. "I've been trying to get Luke to *collect* me for all kinds of things for years and nothing has worked. What do you know that I don't?"

"I have no idea," Maggie said wearily.

"Enjoy your evening, ladies," Luke said, starting down the hallway with Maggie in tow.

Just as Maggie and Luke reentered the main room, a song ended and the band paused, then began to play a slow, dreamy waltz.

"Perfect," Luke said, smiling as he led Maggie onto the crowded, gleaming floor.

And then Maggie was in Luke's embrace, swaying to the music as though they had spent a lifetime dancing together. He nestled her close to his body and she totally ignored the naggy little voice in her mind that was telling her she was in a danger zone, should move backward, keep space between them.

"Mmm," Luke said, "you smell so nice. What kind of perfume is that?"

"Soap," Maggie said.

Luke chuckled and the sexy sound caused Maggie to shiver.

"Are you cold?" Luke said, pulling her even closer.

Maggie's breasts were crushed to the hard wall of Luke's chest in a sweet pain that made her acutely aware of her femininity in contrast to his blatant maleness. Heat swirled within her, finally pulsing low in her body.

"No. I'm…I'm definitely not cold."

"You feel so good in my arms, Maggie. Perfect, absolutely perfect."

"Well…" Maggie started, then for the life of her couldn't think of one intelligent thing to say.

And the music played on.

The crowd surrounding them disappeared, along with the buzz of conversation from those on the sidelines who weren't dancing. The room itself no longer existed. It was just the two of them and the music, encased in a sensual mist.

Ah, Maggie, Luke thought. He wanted this dance to last forever. Holding Maggie in his arms was heaven in its purest form. She fit against him as though she'd been custom-made. Well, that was actually true. Yes, custom-made just for him because she was his other half, and he loved her with an intensity that was beyond description.

They were dancing like Cinderella and the prince at the ball, Luke mentally rambled on. But in that fairy tale it all fell apart at the stroke of midnight. That poor slob of a prince was left with empty arms and an aching heart, wondering if he'd ever see his newfound love again.

Well, that wasn't going to happen to Luke St. John, damn it. No way. Because he was going to come up with a rock-solid plan that would enable him to see Maggie on a regular basis without running the risk of her turning him down.

But how in hell was he going to do that?

Where was this genius-level plan going to come from? He'd searched his brain for it until he was exhausted, and it wasn't there, he'd come up empty.

Think, St. John. His entire future happiness depended on that unknown plan.

The song ended.

No, Luke thought frantically. Not yet.

"Luke?" Maggie looked up at him as they stopped moving, realizing that he had not relinquished his hold on her one iota.

"Yes?"

"Could we dance to just one more song?"

"Yes," he said. They would dance to a lifetime of songs played just for them. "It will be my pleasure."

Another waltz began and they swayed to the lilting music.

What on earth had possessed her to ask Luke to dance with her again? Maggie thought, feeling a flush of embarrassment warm her cheeks. How brazen was that, for Pete's sake? Not only brazen but dumb, really dumb. She was supposed to be putting distance between them, not practically begging to be kept nestled close, so enticingly close, to his body.

But he felt so good and smelled so good and he danced so smoothly she was transformed into Ginger Rogers. Oh, what harm could one more dance do? She'd never see Luke again after tonight, so why not have the memory of two fantasy-filled dances instead of just one? Sure, why not?

It was sort of like the story of Cinderella, only this handsome prince wasn't going to run all over the kingdom of Phoenix trying on a shoe to find her. No this was it, all there would be, and the very thought of that was so depressing it was enough to make her weep buckets.

Soon—much, much too soon—the song ended. Maggie drew a steadying breath, then stepped back out of Luke's arms.

"Thank you," she said, smiling slightly. "That was lovely. I... Well, I have things to check on regarding the cleanup crew and what have you so... It was nice meeting you, Luke. Goodbye."

"Good night, Maggie," he said quietly.

Maggie made her way through the crowd on the dance floor, and Luke watched her go before weaving through the guests to return to the head table. He sat down next to his father, a distinguished-looking man with a trim build and salt-and-pepper hair.

"Everything went very well this evening, don't you think?" Mason St. John said. "Your brother and Ginger must be pleased."

"Mmm." Luke rocked his chair back on two legs and folded his arms over his chest.

"Your mother is still out there dancing," his father continued. "She's having a marvelous time."

"Mmm."

"The wedding cake was the best I've ever tasted,"

Mason said. "Some I've had over the years have been like sawdust with a plastic bride and groom on top."

"Mmm."

"I do believe you've met your match in Maggie Jenkins, son," Mason said. "You have all the signs of a man who has had the pins knocked out from under him."

"Mmm," Luke said, then blinked and thudded the chair back onto four legs. "What?"

Mason chuckled. "I thought that might get your attention. I've been watching you, Luke. You're a goner. I was beginning to believe there wasn't a woman in Phoenix who could stake a claim on you, but Maggie Jenkins obviously has. What I don't understand is why you look so gloomy."

"It's very simple, Dad," Luke said. "Maggie may plan fantastic weddings but she doesn't want one for herself. She has no intention of marrying. I don't know if you believe in love at first sight, but it has happened to me big-time. I am irrevocably in love with a woman who wants no part of 'until death do us part.'"

"Well, for the record," Mason said, "I certainly do believe in love at first sight. I fell in love with your mother when we were in the seventh grade and one of the rubber bands from her braces flew off and smacked me right in the eye. As for your Maggie? It doesn't take a genius to figure out that you need a plan."

"Oh, man," Luke said, squeezing the bridge of his nose, "don't say that word. I've worn out my brain already trying to come up with exactly that—a plan. And I'm running on empty.

"Maggie isn't going to go for the wine-and-dine routine. No way. She'd head for the hills before she got tangled up in anything that even hinted of courtship, a serious relationship. I can literally see, feel, the walls she's built around herself."

"So chip away at them. That's where the plan comes in," Mason said. "Come on, Luke. You're a St. John. We go for the gusto, we're winners, we don't even entertain the word *defeat*."

"In the courtroom," Luke said. "Dealing with women is a whole different arena, Dad. It calls for understanding the female mind, and I'm not sure there's a man on this planet who can do that."

"Good point. I certainly don't know what makes those wonderful creatures tick, even after all these years," Mason said, stroking his chin. "Well, now, this is going to be quite a challenge for you, isn't it?"

"The most important fight of my life," Luke said. "I really, *really* need an idea."

"Yep," Mason said, nodding. "Keep me posted on this, son."

"Yeah, okay. In the meantime, pass that champagne bottle down here, will you? Maybe there's a magic answer waiting for me in the bubbly."

Mason laughed as he handed his son the bottle. "All that is in there is a hangover waiting to happen."

"Whatever," Luke said, then filled his glass to the brim.

Late the next morning Luke rolled onto his back in bed, opened his eyes and groaned. He closed his eyes again, pressed his hand to his throbbing forehead, then dropped his arms to the bed with a thud.

He was a dying man, he thought, eyes still tightly closed. Some idiot was playing a bongo drum in this brain, every tooth in his mouth ached and even his hair hurt. To even hope to survive he'd have to cut off his head and grow a new one.

"Ohhh, I hate champagne," he said aloud, with another groan thrown in for good measure. "I'm never drinking that junk again. This is somehow all Maggie Jenkins's fault, damn it."

Luke opened his eyes slowly, then eased upward and moved his feet cautiously to the floor. He propped his elbows on his knees and cradled his throbbing head in his hands.

He couldn't believe he'd done this, he thought miserably. He hadn't gotten smashed since his freshman year in college many years ago. But there he'd sat, filling his glass with expensive champagne, chugging it down, filling it again and again and again.

He vaguely remembered his father watching him and chuckling with maddening regularity, then finally extending his hand and asking for Luke's car keys.

So how had he gotten home? Oh, yeah, his dad had driven him with his mother following in their vehicle. Well, at least his SUV must be parked in the garage beneath the building. His mother had seemed to get a kick out of her oldest son's condition, too, now that he thought about it. What rotten parents.

At least Robert didn't know what his big brother had

done. Robert and Ginger had changed into their traveling clothes and with all the proper fuss had left the reception to catch the plane to their honeymoon in Greece.

Their honeymoon. Because they had just gotten married. Mr. and Mrs. Robert St. John. Robert and Ginger were so happy it was nauseating. No, that wasn't fair. He was sincerely pleased that Robert had found his happiness in ditzy Ginger. By this time next year they would no doubt have produced the first St. John grandchild. How crummy was that?

"Knock it off," Luke said, the sound of his own voice increasing the pain in his head.

He was so jealous of Robert and Ginger, it was a crime. And envious of his parents and every other dewy-eyed in-love couple on the face of the earth.

Well, watch out world, because Luke St. John was in love, too, and…and had gotten as drunk as a skunk because the woman of his heart wasn't remotely close to being in love with him. What a bummer.

Luke staggered to his feet, steadied, then shuffled into the bathroom, where he stood under a very hot shower for a very long time. He dressed in jeans and a T-shirt, consumed four cups of coffee with four matching aspirins and decided he might, just might, live.

He wandered into the living room and slouched onto the large sofa, resting his head on the top and staring at the ceiling.

How many people, he wondered, would decide to take the big step and get married after witnessing the faultless Barrington-St. John wedding Maggie had produced the night before? Would her phone be ringing off the hook Monday morning with newly engaged brides-to-be? That was sure what *he* would like to be doing come the first of the week—helping to plan the wedding of all weddings and...

Luke sat bolt upward, then smacked one hand against his forehead as the sudden motion caused a lightning bolt to shoot through his head.

There it is, he thought, his hear racing. Even through the last lingering fog of his hangover it was taking shape, coming together, clicking into place.

The Plan.

"Yes," he said, punching one fist high in the air.

Maggie spent Sunday catching up on Roses and Wishes paperwork, tackling a mound of laundry and cleaning her neglected apartment on the upper floor of the old house.

That done, she shopped for groceries for her Mother Hubbard cupboards. She prepared a nice dinner for herself of baked chicken, mashed potatoes and gravy and a fruit salad, with the smug knowledge that the effort would provide enough leftovers for several days.

What she did *not* do was think.

Upon waking that morning she'd made a firm vow that she would not dwell on the subject of Luke St. John. Not relive the kiss at the altar during the rehearsal or the dances they'd shared.

No remembrances would be allowed of the heated sensations that had consumed her when Luke's lips had captured hers and while she had been held so tightly in his arms during the dreamy waltzes.

She'd shoo away any images that threatened to creep into her mental vision of Luke's deep brown eyes, his thick beckoning-to-her-fingers hair, his wide shoulders and those incredible strong but gentle hands of his.

Through the entire day she concentrated on her chores and kept busy, busy, busy, becoming extremely proud of herself for her restraint and self-control.

Luke and the success of the Barrington-St. John wedding were now old news, done, finished, kaput, and her thoughts were directed toward the start of the fresh week at Roses and Wishes. She focused on the hope that new business from all those cards she'd seen tucked away at the reception would cause the phone to ring off the hook.

She mentally patted herself on the back for doing such a stellar job of keeping her vow. The day had gone exactly as she'd planned.

But then she ran out of things to do.

She had spit-shined the kitchen after dinner, taken a leisurely bubble bath in her super-duper tub, then settled onto the sofa in an old-fashioned, pale pink, soft cotton granny nightgown that was perfect for the warm summer night.

Glancing at the little clock on the end table, she frowned when she saw that it was only a few minutes after eight o'clock. She was tired from her nonstop day but not sleepy enough to go to bed.

"Television," she said, snatching up the remote.

She channel surfed three times, sighed, then turned off the TV realizing there was just nothing on that she wanted to watch.

"Read a book," she said, grabbing a paperback novel on the coffee table.

After reading the same page four times and having no idea what it said, she plunked the book back onto the table and glared at it.

She wiggled into a more comfortable position on the rather lumpy sofa, crossed her arms over her breasts and stared into space.

And thought of Luke St. John.

"This is dumb, dumb, dumb," she said with a cluck of self-disgust.

Well, she thought, maybe not. Perhaps she was approaching this all wrong. Granted, she'd kept Luke at bay during the hours of the day, but she couldn't continue such a frenzied schedule or she'd collapse into an exhausted heap on the floor.

So. New idea. She *would* indulge in dwelling on all that had transpired between her and Luke, *would* allow images of his masculine magnificence to consume her mind, *would* invite the womanly sensual sensations to once again swirl and churn and burn within her. Then she'd wrap all those things up like a precious treasure and tuck them away in a secret chamber of her heart and be done with them for all time. The end.

"Very good," she said with a decisive nod. "Go for it, Maggie."

And she did.

And spent a long night tossing and turning in her bed, alternating between hot waves of overpowering desire and the chill of loneliness.

Late the next morning Maggie sat in the office of Roses and Wishes and stared gloomily at the telephone, which had not rung once since she'd come downstairs.

Well, that was fine, she rationalized. It didn't mean she wasn't going to garner any new business from the success of the Barrington-St. John wedding. She was being much too impatient, that's all. Brides-to-be had to come back to earth from cloud nine and start thinking about what kind of wedding they wished to have. They'd mentally sift and sort, mull it over, then eventually call Roses and Wishes to set things in motion. Sure.

Maggie left the office and went into the reception area, where she straightened albums that didn't need straightening, dusted what wasn't dusty. She switched two easy chairs to opposite sides of the love seat, then put them back where they'd been.

With a sigh she trudged back into the office, sank onto the chair behind the desk and, for lack of anything better to do, doodled on a legal pad and munched on yogurt-covered almonds.

She was tired, she mused, and that was Luke St. John's fault. She'd given him several hours of her evening last night, but she'd certainly not invited him into her bed and the dreams she'd had when she'd finally managed to doze off. Pushy, rude man. He'd refused to stay beyond her bedroom door as ordered, darn it.

The bell over the front door jingled, indicating someone had entered the house, and Maggie jumped to her feet, nearly tipping over the chair in the process.

She told herself to get a professional grip, for heaven's sake, took a steadying breath as she smoothed her pale blue top over the waistband of her white slacks and actually managed to walk to the main area in a fairly slow, ladylike manner.

Then stopped dead and forgot to breathe.

"Hello, Maggie," Luke St. John said from where he stood just inside the door.

This was absurd, Maggie thought, taking a gulp of much-needed air. Luke wasn't really standing there looking incredibly gorgeous in jeans and an open-necked gray dress shirt. She'd conjured up his image from the wanton section of her brain that insisted on reliving all the sensationally sensuous... This was ridiculous.

"Maggie?" Luke closed the distance between them and frowned. "Hello?"

"You're not here," she said, flapping one hand in the air. "Poof. You're gone." She paused, waited, then tentatively pressed one fingertip to Luke's imaginary chest, which was definitely hard as a rock. Her eyes widened as she stared up at him. "Oh, my gosh, you really are here. Why are you here?"

Luke folded his arms across his chest and stared down at the floor, his shoulders shaking with muffled laughter.

Oh, man, he thought, how he loved this woman. She was obviously jangled by his unexpected arrival at

Roses and Wishes, and that was good news. Great news. If he hadn't had an impact on Maggie, she wouldn't give a damn if he suddenly popped into her place of business.

She was flustered and didn't know how to hide it, and that was so endearing. Maggie was genuine and honest. He wanted to take her into his arms and…

"Mr. St. John?" Maggie said, planting her hands on her hips. "May I help you?"

"I'm beyond help," he said, meeting her gaze with merriment dancing in his brown eyes.

"Pardon me?"

"Never mind." Luke forced a serious expression onto his face. "Yes, you may assist me, Ms. Jenkins. I am in desperate need of your expertise."

This was it, he thought, feeling a sudden trickle of sweat run down his chest. He was putting The Plan into motion. And it would work. It *had* to work.

"My expertise?" Maggie said, cocking her head slightly to one side. "About what?"

"Weddings. I am responsible for planning a wedding, every detail, beginning to end. No expense spared."

Dear heaven, no, Maggie thought, feeling the color drain from her face. Luke St. John was getting married. How could he do such a thing? He hadn't even brought a date to his brother's wedding, for crying out loud. And crying out loud was what she was about to do, because she could feel the tears stinging at the back of her eyes and…

"Are you all right?" Luke said, frowning. "You're very pale all of a sudden. Why don't we sit down on this nice love seat you have?"

"*I'll* sit on the love seat," she said, shooting him a dark look, "and *you* sit on that easy chair."

Luke raised both hands palms out. "No problem. Whatever makes you comfortable."

Once seated, Maggie directed her attention to an invisible piece of lint on one of her knees.

"I must say, Luke," she said, wishing her voice sounded steadier than the quivering little noise she was hearing, "that I'm surprised by your announcement. I mean, you didn't have a…a companion with you at Ginger and Robert's wedding or…

"What did you do? Put all your women's names in a hat, pull one out and decide to marry her because your brother is obviously so happy, so what the heck, why not?" She paused. "Sorry. That was rude. Very rude." She cleared her throat. "So. You wish to hire me—Roses and Wishes—to coordinate your wedding. I appreciate your confidence. It is a bit unusual that you're tending to this and not your bride-to-be, as it's traditional that the woman… Forget that. To each his own. How many people are you going to invite?"

Luke propped one ankle on his other knee and smiled pleasantly. "A lot."

"Could you be a tad more specific?"

"Not at the moment. Just go with a lot for now."

"And when do you plan to have this life-changing event?" Maggie said, looking over at him.

"The sooner the better," he said. "But I'm not exactly sure at this point in time."

"I see." Maggie frowned. "No, I don't. Call me stupid, but this isn't making one bit of sense. You want me to coordinate a wedding for a lot, number unknown, of guests, and it's to be held the sooner the better, but you don't have a clue as to when."

Luke nodded. "That's it in a nutshell."

A rather hysterical giggle escaped from Maggie's lips. "Do you know anything for certain? Like, for example, who the bride is?"

"Oh, yes, ma'am," he said. "That is etched in stone."

"How nice," she said miserably. "What I mean is… I'm not sure what I mean. This is very confusing."

"It is?" Luke said, an expression of pure innocence on his face. "I need a wedding planned, you're a wedding planner—coordinator, whatever." He shrugged. "Seems to me I've come to the right place, especially after seeing what a dynamite job you did for Ginger and Robert."

"But Ginger knew what she wanted and when she wanted it," Maggie said, throwing up her hands. "Well, sort of. She did change her mind about a ton of things, but generally speaking, she knew. You know—three hundred, give or take, guests, a summer wedding, seven bridesmaids, yogurt-covered almonds in the nut cups, details like that."

"Oh," Luke said, nodding. "Well, I don't know any of that stuff. Except forget the almonds. I don't like almonds, yogurt-covered or otherwise."

"Oh, well, with that data I'm ready to roll," Maggie said, throwing up her hands again. "No almonds in the nut cups." She shook her head. "This is insane."

"Tell me this, Maggie," Luke said, leaning toward her. "How long does it take to put on a production like Ginger and Robert's shindig?"

"At least six months," she said, "and that's going full speed ahead."

"Really? That long? Grim, very grim. Well, if that's the best you can do… Okay, let's aim for a Christmas wedding. How's that?"

Sure, Maggie thought, feeling the threat of tears again. Merry Christmas to Maggie Jenkins. She could watch Luke St. John get married. Hooray.

Darn it, what difference did it make? Why was she falling apart because Luke suddenly realized he was in love with one of the high-society women he dated and wanted to get married and live happily ever after? It had nothing to do with her beyond being a real coup for Roses and Wishes.

So why did she feel so sad?

Why did she want to crawl into bed and cry for a week?

Forget it, just forget it. She wasn't talking to herself about this anymore because she was being absolutely, positively ridiculous.

"Maggie?" Luke said. "Does that work for you? A Christmas wedding?"

"Yes," she said softly as she looked at a spot in space a couple of inches above Luke's head. "A Christmas wedding will be just fine, very beautiful and…special. Definitely a Christmas to remember forever."

Five

Luke nodded and rubbed his hands together. "Actually this schedule will work out perfectly. A holiday wedding. That's really romantic, don't you think?"

"What? Uh, yes, very romantic," Maggie said with a rather wistful sigh as she shifted her gaze to the opposite wall. "It's a magical time of year as it is. And to be getting married then, too? Goodness, that's over the top or however you want to put it."

"Yep." Luke paused and looked at Maggie intently. "I'll tell…*them*…the good news."

Maggie snapped her head around to stare at Luke. "Them? Them who?" She paused. "You mean the families?"

"Nooo," Luke said slowly. "I was referring to the bride and groom."

"Pardon me?" she said, obviously confused.

"Oh," Luke said, snapping his fingers, "I didn't make myself clear on this at all, did I? I do apologize, Maggie. The wedding we're discussing is for my cousin and his fiancée."

"What?" Maggie blinked. "You mean *you're* not... What?"

"Let me start at the top," Luke said, lacing his fingers on his chest. "My cousin...Clyde..."

Jeez, what a name, he thought, inwardly groaning. He should have given thought to the identity of these people before he got here. The bride, the bride. What was the bride's name?

He looked frantically around the room, his gaze falling on the cover of a thick photograph album imprinted with the words *Precious Memories* in gold.

"...and the love of his life...Precious," he went on, "are in London working for the State Department."

"Clyde and Precious?" Maggie said, raising her eyebrows.

"Yep, good ol' cousin Clyde. Anyway, they decided they'd best get married here in Phoenix to keep the families from murdering them. However, they agreed to stay on in their positions as long as possible to train their replacements before returning to the States.

"They did stipulate to their boss, though, that they definitely wanted to be back home for the holidays. So, you see, a wedding at that time of year keeps everybody happy. Are you happy, Maggie?"

"I'm ecstatic," she said, smiling. Because Luke wasn't getting married. He wasn't. Thank goodness, because... Because why? She didn't know, but there was no denying that the dark cloud that had settled over her was gone, poof, just disappeared, because Luke wasn't talking about *his* wedding. "Ecstatic because... Yes, because this is wonderful news for...for Roses and Wishes."

"Of course," Luke said, nodding. "Now let me make something very clear. Precious is a rather unusual young woman. She'd much prefer to just go to City Hall in her jeans and marry her beloved Clyde, but the mothers would freak and Clyde and Precious would never hear the end of it.

"So when I spoke with them on the phone yesterday I suggested that they hire you to arrange the whole she-bang and all they have to do is show up. They're thrilled. Precious said she'd go along with any decisions you make. Clyde? Hey, guys don't care about this kind of stuff. It's a woman thing."

"You mean I get to plan the whole wedding, make it the way I want it to be and... What about the mothers? The mothers will never let me do that. They'll want to step in and put this production together."

"No way," Luke said. "They're as different as day and night, those mothers. My aunt and Precious's mom to-gether are a war waiting to happen. They're not going to know a thing about it.

"They'll get an invitation in the mail, just like everyone else who is invited. They'll pout for a while, I suppose, but then they'll jump right into fast-forward and
start thinking about becoming grandmothers, and all
will be well."

"This is crazy," Maggie said, shaking her head.

"No, this is exactly the way it should be done." Luke
leaned forward, only inches from Maggie as he looked
directly into her eyes. "You pretend this is *your* dream
wedding, Maggie. Make the decisions based on what
you would want if *you* were getting married."

"Oh...my...gracious," Maggie whispered.

"The thing is, Clyde and Precious feel they'd better
be kept up to date on what's what, you know what I
mean? Just in case the moms quiz them later on why
they decided on something. For example, if you have
them get married in a hot-air balloon, they want to be
prepared with a solid story about how they have this
thing for hot-air balloons. Get it?"

"I..."

"Therefore, I'll be sticking pretty close to you
through this whole endeavor so I have all the details
straight to pass along to them as we go. My father will
take up the slack for me at the office to free up some of
my time because Clyde is his favorite nephew. My dad
is semiretired, but for this occasion he's willing to put
in extra hours.

"So I'd say that about covers it. Remember, no expense spared. Oh, and Precious is about your size, so
there shouldn't be any problem about your picking out

her wedding dress—if you want a traditional wedding dress. That's up to you. Any questions?"

"I-I'm stunned," Maggie said, shaking her head. "I'm having difficulty comprehending all this because it's so… I can't even think of a word to describe it."

Try *brilliant,* Luke thought smugly. The Plan was nothing short of brilliant. Maggie would produce the wedding of *her* dreams. He had set it up perfectly to be able to stick close to her through the whole thing and he'd be chipping away at those walls of hers little by little, brick by emotional brick.

She would come to love him, just as he loved her. God, she just had to fall in love with him, want to marry him and spend the rest of her life by his side. *Ah, please, Maggie.*

"Will you do it?" Luke said. "I mean, take on this project?"

"Well, yes, of course I will. Yes."

"Great. That's even more than great. Thank you, Maggie, from the bottom of my heart. I'm really grateful. That is, Clyde and Precious will be very grateful to you for doing this." Luke paused. "I realize that you don't wish to ever marry, but that doesn't mean you haven't thought about the kind of wedding you'd like to have if you intended to marry, even though you don't…intend to marry. Right? Did that make sense?"

"I think so," Maggie said, frowning slightly. "Yes, I understand what you said. And I suppose I do wonder about how I would do things each time I coordinate a wedding. It's human nature, you know what I mean?

"For example, when Ginger finally settled on pale yellow as one of her colors, I couldn't help feeling that with so many blond bridesmaids a deeper shade would have been more striking. Of course, I didn't say that to Ginger, but I *was* thinking it."

"There you go," Luke said, nodding. "That's exactly what I was referring to. Have you ever put together a holiday wedding before?"

"No."

"Then you won't be influenced by a previous bride's choices. The decisions will be exclusively yours." Luke beamed. "Won't that be fun?"

"I…"

"You're not scheduled to do another wedding right away, are you?" Luke said. "You're free to concentrate totally on Clyde and Precious's do?"

"Their wedding will have Roses and Wishes' undivided attention," Maggie said, smiling.

"Great." Luke frowned. "Mmm. The church. Which one would you pick?"

"Me? Well, I happen to be Episcopalian, but—"

"Terrific. You can book the same church that Ginger and Robert had. That will suit Clyde and Precious just fine."

"Well, sure. Okay. Goodness, my head is spinning. This is rather overwhelming because it's so…strange. What about bridesmaids? The dresses have to be custom-fitted, you know."

Oops, Luke thought. Quick, St. John, come up with a solution to that.

"Well," he said slowly. "Who would you choose as your attendants?"

"Me? My sister and my best friend."

"That's all? Just two?"

Maggie laughed. "Not everyone has seven bridesmaids like Ginger, Luke."

"True," he said. "Two. I'll pass that on to Precious. Why don't you find out what size dresses your two choices wear, and the seamstress or whatever you call her can adjust to the size of Precious's bridesmaids."

"Well, it's not perfect, but it might work if there's time enough to nip and tuck before the actual wedding—provided, of course, that everyone is at least close to matching in size. My sister Janet wears a twelve. My best friend Patty is a ten."

"And you?"

"Me? I wear a size eight."

"Got it. I'll double-check all three of those numbers with Precious." Luke paused. "There. Problem solved. We're a good team, Maggie Jenkins." Luke looked directly into Maggie's big brown eyes. "A very good team. You. Me. Together."

"Together," Maggie whispered as she stared into Luke's mesmerizing eyes.

She was about to start planning her fantasy wedding, Maggie mused dreamily. The one she would never have but had thought about so very much. And Luke St. John would be beside her every step of the way, as though he was the groom and she was the bride and... This was totally bizarre.

And very, very dangerous.

She had to keep herself grounded in reality through the months ahead, not get emotionally caught up in what she and Luke were doing. It was an unusual project assigned to Roses and Wishes, that's all.

The bride was Precious, the groom was Clyde. She must remember that at all times. And keeping her head and heart straight would be a lot easier if she quit gazing into those compelling eyes of Luke's.

"Well," Maggie said much too loudly and causing Luke to jerk at her sudden outburst, "this has certainly been an interesting meeting." She got to her feet. "As the owner of Roses and Wishes, I'd like to sincerely thank you for your confidence in me to coordinate the perfect wedding for Precious and Clyde."

"You're welcome," Luke said, rising. "Just out of curiosity, what will you do first?"

"Select the colors. There are so many things—details, details, details—that have to tie into them that it's important they are chosen early on." Maggie laughed. "The way Ginger kept changing her mind about her colors was nerve-racking, to say the least."

"You won't have to worry about that type of thing this time, will you?" Luke said, smiling. "You're planning *your* wedding—so to speak."

"Well, yes, so to speak. But not really. Well, sort of, because whatever I decide is how it will be. But then again... Never mind. It's going to take a while to adjust to such a once-in-a-lifetime endeavor."

"That's what weddings should be, don't you think?"

Luke said quietly. "A once-in-a-lifetime, forever-and-ever event for the bride and groom?"

"Of course." Maggie sighed. "But in today's society the forever-and-ever part doesn't mean much to some couples."

"There hasn't been a divorce in our family," Luke said, "for as far back as anyone can remember."

Maggie's eyes widened. "You're kidding. That's amazing."

"Not really," Luke said, shaking his head. "I believe that St. Johns are just very good at listening to their hearts, knowing what is right and real and falling in love with someone who is on the same wavelength. My dad fell in love with my mother when they were in the seventh grade. I kid you not, it's true."

"Awesome," Maggie said. "That's a rather dopey word to use, but it fits. Seventh grade? And there hasn't been even one divorce in your family history? Totally awesome. Almost unbelievable. You don't suppose some of those couples stayed together even though they were miserable because they didn't want to be the first to break that magical spell, do you?"

"Nope," Luke said. "No way. A stranger seeing any of my family with their partners would be able to tell that they're deeply in love. Ginger and Robert will grow old together and be just as happy as they were at their wedding. So will…Precious and Clyde. Yeah, so will Precious and Clyde."

"That's so beautiful," Maggie said wistfully.

"What about *your* family, Maggie?"

She frowned. "We're..." She mumbled something that wasn't quite clear.

"Pardon me?" Luke said, frowning.

"Never mind," she said quickly. "Well, I have my work cut out for me, don't I? And the first order of business is choosing colors for a Christmas wedding."

"I'll leave you to get started on the plans," Luke said, "but I'll be in touch very soon. Goodbye for now, Maggie, and thank you."

"Oh, I thank you, Luke. Goodbye."

As Luke closed the door behind him, Maggie sank onto the love seat and drew a steadying breath as she continued to digest all that had just happened. Then she shifted her gaze to the center of the table that held the albums.

It had been her plan when she'd opened Roses and Wishes, she thought, to always have a vase of roses, her very favorite flower, right there in that spot. She soon realized, however, that the budget would not allow for such an extravagance.

Roses. She would carry... No, no, *Precious* would carry a bouquet of red roses with baby's breath and Christmas greenery all tied together with one red and one white satin ribbon.

She'd named her fledgling business Roses and Wishes because it held a secret meaning for her. Her wishes were simple but not hers to have. A husband, children, a home. Life with a man who loved her as much as she loved him.

Roses. She'd be a bride who carried roses down the

aisle and later grew them in the garden behind the home she shared with her family.

Roses and Wishes. She'd wanted that name where she could see it, her attempt to find fulfillment in helping brides make their wishes come true. Well, this time she got to go one step further. She had chosen roses for the bridal bouquet. Gorgeous, fragrant red roses.

Maggie smiled and leaned her head back on the back of the love seat.

The colors must be chosen for this Christmas wedding, she mused. Well, it really wasn't that difficult. Red roses. And the attendants would wear rich forest-green satin dresses with shoes to match. They would carry bouquets of red and white baby carnations.

The taper candles that would be used to light the one signifying a single entity would be white and the center candle would be red.

And her dress? It would be white as freshly fallen snow, simple but elegant, with a train and a frothy veil— a veil that Luke would lift at the proper moment to kiss his bride and…

"No," Maggie said, jumping to her feet. "Stop it right now. Back up and get it right, Maggie Jenkins."

Precious's dress. Precious's veil. Clyde's kiss for his new wife. This was Precious and Clyde's wedding she was coordinating.

"Thank you," she said, dropping back down on the love seat. "That's better. Don't make that mistake again, Ms. Jenkins. Not once in the months ahead while you tend to the details, details, details."

* * *

As Luke maneuvered his SUV through the heavy Phoenix traffic, he made no attempt to curb the wide smile on his face.

He'd done it, he thought, tapping his fingertip on the steering wheel. He'd set his brilliant plan in motion and it had worked, it had actually worked. Maggie was now committed to coordinating a fantastic wedding for his imaginary cousin Clyde and the ever-famous Precious. Man, he really should have given thought to names for the bride and groom before he'd gone to Roses and Wishes. Oh, well.

Back to The Plan. Maggie would create the wedding of her dreams. *Her* dreams. And if everything went as he hoped and prayed, that wedding would actually take place. Maggie Jenkins would marry Luke St. John at some point during the Christmas holidays.

Of course, there was a long way to go before that ceremony happened. Maggie had to fall in love with him, just as he had with her. She was attracted to him, unsettled by him, was feeling something for him already, he was sure of that.

She had to fall in love with him and trust him enough to be willing to allow him to crumble into dust those protective walls she'd constructed around herself, so he could reach out and take her into his arms…forever.

Yeah, he had his tasks cut out for him, but Maggie was worth fighting for and he intended to win. He *had* to win.

Luke frowned as he suddenly recalled Maggie's

strange response when the conversation had centered on all the happy marriages in his family. He'd asked about her family and—what had she said? She'd sort of mumbled a word and he just wasn't sure what it had been. When he'd pressed, she'd quickly changed the subject.

"Damn," Luke said, smacking the steering wheel with the heel of one hand.

Maybe it was an important clue about Maggie's aversion to getting married, to being determined to plan weddings for other people but never for herself.

He'd said…then she'd said… Oh, hell, what had Maggie said?

Six

That evening Maggie and her best friend Patty sat on the floor in Maggie's minuscule living room eating take-out pizza, sipping sodas and going through a tower of bride magazines page by page.

The two had been friends since elementary school and now, at twenty-five years old, neither could imagine dealing with the ups and downs of life without the other's support.

Patty taught first grade at the same school she and Maggie had attended. Patty's parents had been killed in an automobile accident five years before, so now every spare cent she had went toward putting her younger brother through college.

"Look at this," Patty said, tapping one fingertip on a

page of the magazine in front of her. "Tiny Christmas balls nestled in the bridesmaids' bouquets. Do you like that idea?"

Maggie wrinkled her nose. "It's a bit much, I think. I don't want to overdo the Christmas theme." She laughed. "After all, this is a wedding, hon, not an office party."

"True," Patty said, turning the page. "Forget the icky ornaments." She took another bite of pizza and looked at Maggie. "It's so strange to be sitting here doing this, Maggie. I get so caught up in it, I have to keep reminding myself that we're not really planning *your* wedding."

"I know," Maggie said, sighing, "but this is the closest we'll ever get to actually doing that, so enjoy."

"Don't get me started on that subject," Patty said, shaking her head. "The fact that you won't even consider the possibility of falling in love and getting married because—"

"Patty."

"Okay, okay, I'll shut up." Patty paused. "This whole project is weird. Who ever heard of a bride who didn't give a damn about the plans for her own wedding? Are you sure this Precious person is playing with a full deck?"

Maggie shrugged. "Luke said Precious would just as soon get married wearing jeans at a courthouse. This production is to satisfy the mothers. Mothers I don't have to deal with, which is a blessing. This will be the wedding of…well, *my* dreams. Roses and wishes and…

Anyway, I intend to thoroughly go for it because nothing like this will ever happen again. The only person I have to report to is Luke."

"Luke St. John," Patty said wistfully. "I've seen his picture in the newspaper. He is so gorgeous, he's hot! To think that you actually danced with him at his brother's wedding reception." She stared into space. "To be held in the arms of Luke St. John must have been heaven on earth."

"Close, very close," Maggie said, nodding. "He's a marvelous dancer, made me feel like I was floating on a cloud and…" Sudden heat stained her cheeks a pretty pink. "Forget that. Do you think having the bridesmaids wearing green is corny? Maybe I should start over in my mind and not address the Christmas thing at all."

"Oh, no, don't do that," Patty said. "People will expect a festive touch. Besides, it's what you want. Right?"

"Well, yes."

"Then it's settled. Stay with the Christmas theme, but don't go over the top. What did your sister say about all this?"

"Janet said it was nuts," Maggie said, smiling, "but that she'd be delighted to be fitted for a beautiful dress even if she doesn't get to actually wear it anywhere. As a single mom with three kids, she said they don't provide fittings—la-di-da—in the thrift shops where she buys her clothes."

"How funny." Patty laughed, then frowned. "What

was your mom's reaction? She must think Precious has a screw loose."

"She didn't dwell on Precious's mind-set," Maggie said. "Eat that last piece of pizza. I'm stuffed."

"No problem," she said, reaching for the slice. "So what *did* your mom focus on about this crazy situation?"

"She's worried about me, Patty," Maggie said quietly. "She's afraid that I'll spend all these weeks planning my dream wedding and then fall apart when I have to face the reality of it being for someone else."

She sighed. "In fact, she's concerned about me being a wedding coordinator in the first place. She thinks it was a stupid business for me to start considering I'll never have a wedding of my own. She's afraid I'll spend my life being so sad because I'll be constantly reminded that... Oh, you know."

"What I know," Patty said, shaking her head, "is you won't budge on the subject of your not getting married, and your mom and Janet—and even your brother, for all I know—are on the same wavelength about it. I'm totally outnumbered when it comes to convincing you otherwise."

"So don't try. Heavens, look at this picture in this magazine. The bridal bouquet has green and red candles in it and they're lit, for heaven's sake."

"It boggles the mind," Patty said, laughing. "Talk about being hot. Which brings me back to the subject of Luke St. John. You said he's really nice, not snooty even though he's as rich as Midas?"

"Yes." Maggie nodded. "He's very, very nice."

"And he has a sense of humor and a good relationship with his family and dances like a dream and looks as good in jeans as he does in a tux and... Maggie, you'd better be very careful during the weeks ahead. You're going to be seeing a lot of Luke because of this wedding. Luke sounds like he's capable of smashing hearts to smithereens. I don't want one of those hearts to be yours."

"Believe me, I don't either," Maggie said. "I'm very aware of Luke's...attributes, shall we say. But fear not, because I'm on red alert, the walls are up, the door is barred. There's not a chance on earth that I'll fall head over heels in love with Mr. Luke St. John. Nope. That isn't going to happen."

"And now," Luke said, "I have to make certain that Maggie falls head over heels in love with me."

Mason St. John chuckled. "That's definitely top of the list considering you want to marry Maggie Jenkins, have a slew of little St. Johns, then grow old and creaky together."

"Right," Luke said, then cut a chunk out of the enormous steak on the plate in front of him.

Father and son were dining at Mason's club, which he had yet to convince Luke to join. Luke had made it clear several years before that he'd consider a membership once the private establishment got with the program and allowed women to join.

"I must say, Luke," Mason said after consuming several forkfuls of succulent roast beef, "that I'm impressed with this plan you've come up with. It's brilliant. And I'm more than happy to cover things for you at the office as this scheme unfolds."

"I appreciate that, Dad. Remember, not a word of this to Mom. She couldn't keep a secret if her life depended on it, plus she'd be calling me constantly with advice about how to win Maggie's heart."

"That she would, bless her," Mason said, smiling. "I just wish you'd… Oh, Lord." His shoulders started shaking with laughter as he pressed his napkin to his lips.

Luke frowned. "Don't go there. I thought you were going to get us kicked out of here earlier because you were laughing so loud. Just don't think about it."

"I'm trying not to, but…Clyde and Precious?"

"I forgot to think of names for my fictitious bride and groom before I went to see Maggie. I was under pressure. I realize they're grim but…" Luke shrugged.

"What's Clyde's last name?" Mason said. "Is he a St. John? Clyde St. John." He started laughing again. "I can't handle that."

"Okay, okay. Knock it off. All right, let's see. Clyde's mother is your sister and she married… Who did she marry?"

"John Smith."

"That's really original," Luke said, rolling his eyes heavenward. "All right. Whatever. Clyde Smith is going to marry Precious, um…Peterson."

"Precious Peterson?" Mason said with a hoot of merriment that drew several frowns from other diners. "Sorry. So this extravaganza is the Peterson-Smith wedding. Got it. Having it during the Christmas holidays is a nice touch. Very romantic." He took a sip of wine. "What happens next?"

"I wait for Maggie to make some decisions and contact me so I can pass on the data to Precious and Clyde. Well, Precious at least. Clyde will go along with things just like any other groom would. Your favorite nephew is a laid-back, go-with-the-flow guy."

"Ah," Mason said, nodding.

"I have to concentrate on Maggie, chip away at those barriers of hers, get her to allow herself to fall in love with me."

"Ah."

"There's a special…something…already happening between Maggie and me, Dad, I know there is. It's rare, important, real. You should have seen her face when she thought I wanted her to plan my wedding to some other woman. She tried to hide it, but she was upset, I know she was. When I finally told her that it was cousin Clyde's wedding, she just lit up. She feels something for me, she cares. I have to nurture that, make it grow, get her to trust me, come to love me as I love her, then agree to be my wife for all time."

"Ah."

Luke glared at his father. "Can't you say anything else besides 'ah'? A little advice would be helpful here, you know."

Mason set his fork and knife on the edge of his plate, folded his arms over his chest and looked at his son.

"Love is very complicated," Mason said quietly. "But

at the same time it's very simple." He shook his head. "It's hard to explain. You construct a sturdy foundation together and build on that as the years go by. One of the bricks in that foundation, Luke, is honesty. Your plan to win Maggie's heart is based on duplicity."

"But—"

"I know, I know," Mason said, raising one hand. "You're convinced that if you try to court Maggie, she'll refuse to see you, won't run the risk of finding herself in a serious relationship. I understand the need for this plan you've come up with. The thing is, will Maggie understand when she knows the truth? Women don't like to be duped. This whole thing could backfire on you."

"You're thoroughly depressing me," Luke said, leaning back in his chair.

"Well, in all fairness, I don't see where you have any choice but to do it this way," Mason continued. "The usual wine-and-dine scenario is not going to work with your young lady, so you've been forced to come up with an alternative approach. A very clever one, I might add."

He chuckled. "Except for the names! I want you to be happy, Luke. I hope your dream for a life with Maggie becomes your reality, I really do."

"Thanks, Dad. This plan will work. It has to. A future without Maggie is not something I'm willing to accept. I'm going to win the heart, the love, of Maggie Jenkins."

At one o'clock the next afternoon Maggie entered a popular downtown restaurant and immediately scooted into the ladies' room. She stood in front of the long mirror above the half dozen sinks and glared at her reflection.

She was nervous, she thought, and furious at herself because she was. Luke had called her early that morning and asked if it would be too much trouble for her to meet him for lunch.

He was waiting for a scheduled long-distance call regarding a case he was about to wrap up and couldn't leave the office to come to Roses and Wishes. The afternoon was jam-packed with bringing his father up to date on Luke's ongoing cases.

He'd spoken with Clyde and Precious, Luke had told her, and wanted to pass on the information he had and blah, blah, blah.

"Oh, sure," Maggie said, still glowering at her image. "Lunch? *Do* lunch? No problem."

Right, she thought dismally. No problem, except for the fact that she was a nervous wreck. That was so dumb. Dumber than dumb. Luke was a client of hers, of Roses and Wishes, nothing more. They were working together to coordinate the wedding of his cousin Clyde and the bride-to-be Precious. The end.

The really humiliating part was that she knew why she was shaky about seeing Luke. Last night she'd had the most sensuous dream imaginable about the two of them. Goodness. She'd wakened in the night all…all hot and bothered, and try as she may she couldn't erase the pictures in her mind of a naked Luke reaching for a naked her, taking her into his naked arms and…

"Stop it." Maggie spun around and stomped out of the ladies' room. "You are just so ridiculous."

She gave her name to the hostess and was immediately shown to a table at the far end of the large room. Luke stood as he saw her coming.

Thank the Lord, Maggie thought giddily, he has his clothes on. Nice suit. Very lawyer-looking suit. Did she look frumpy in white slacks and a flowered blouse? She should have worn a skirt or dress but hadn't wanted to arrive there with naked legs and… Oh, God, she was totally losing it.

"Hello, Maggie," Luke said, smiling, when she reached the table. "It's nice to see you."

Maggie's eyes widened. "See me?" She shook her head slightly and slid onto her chair. "Yes, of course, nice to see me. It's nice to…see you, too, Luke. I really like that suit you're wearing. Excellent suit. I'm *so* glad you're wearing that suit."

Luke frowned. "Are you all right?"

"What? Oh, yes, of course, I am." Maggie busied herself spreading the linen napkin on her lap. "I just didn't sleep very well last night and—" she looked at Luke again "—I'm hungry."

"Well, we can fix that easily enough." Luke signaled to the waitress. "Order whatever you'd like."

The waitress appeared at the table. Maggie ordered the first thing she saw on the menu and told herself to get a grip. Luke asked for a steak sandwich and home fries.

"I really appreciate your coming all the way downtown," Luke said as the waitress hurried off.

"Not a problem," Maggie said. "Did you receive the call you were waiting for?"

"Call? Oh. Yes. Right on schedule." Luke took a sip of water.

Man, I'm crummy at this cloak-and-dagger stuff, he thought. He'd nearly forgotten about his imaginary "appointment" with the telephone. He'd decided to push his luck and attempt to meet with Maggie somewhere other than at Roses and Wishes. The long-distance call had been a great idea, but he'd blow it big-time if he didn't remember what he'd told her.

"What was it you wanted to discuss with me about your conversation with Precious and Clyde?" Maggie said.

"Why don't we enjoy our lunch first, then get into all that after we eat," he said, smiling.

"But you said you have a very busy afternoon," Maggie said.

"Yes, so I do," Luke said, frowning. *Really* crummy at this. "All right. Precious and Clyde will be arriving in Phoenix in the middle of December, so the holiday wedding is great. Right on the money."

Maggie smiled. "Good. I've chosen the flowers and the color of the bridesmaids' dresses with a Christmas theme in mind. Did you ask Precious about her dress size and those of her friends?"

"They're exactly the same as yours, your sister's and your best friend's."

"Isn't that something?" Maggie said. "Then it will just be a matter of nip and tuck."

"Indeed."

Their lunch arrived and Maggie was amazed to find that she'd ordered grilled salmon and steamed vegetables, which weren't exactly her favorite foods but would do in a pinch.

"Now then," Luke said after they'd taken the edge off their appetites. "Clyde and Precious said that they will have just made that long flight from London a couple of weeks before the wedding. They'd prefer to not have to pack their suitcases again and go winging off on a honeymoon right away, which makes sense."

Maggie cocked her head slightly to one side. "They don't want a honeymoon?"

Get this right, fumble-brain, Luke ordered himself. He wanted to plan that oh-so-important honeymoon trip with Maggie when she was engaged to marry him. It was something that they should do together for real, not as part of this charade.

"They'll have a trip later on," he said, narrowing his eyes in concentration. "So what they want is a honeymoon suite here in Phoenix for a few days following the wedding."

Maggie nodded slowly. "I understand. Well, I really don't know what's available because my couples have always left town after the reception. I'll visit some honeymoon suites in the posh hotels and report back to you."

"I thought I'd do that investigating with you," Luke said. "I'll have the time once I bring my father up to speed on my cases at the office, and as the old saying goes, two heads are better than one. You don't mind if I tag along, do you?"

A teenage boy appeared at the table at that moment to refill their water glasses, and Maggie fought the urge to jump up and hug him for giving her a moment to gather her racing thoughts before answering Luke's question.

Visit honeymoon suites with Luke St. John? she mentally repeated. *Honeymoon* suites, where people did what she and Luke had been about to do in her wanton dream? That was not a good idea at all. No, it was a bad plan. Bad, bad. And dumb and dangerous and—

"Maggie?"

But what reasonable excuse could she dish out to Luke as to why he shouldn't come along on the honeymoon-suite tour? she asked herself frantically. Sorry, Mr. You Melt My Bones, but there's a very good chance I might tear your clothes off in one of those romantic suites and get you naked as a jaybird, just like in my dream? Yeah, right, she'd just lay that on him. Not.

"Maggie, are you with me here?" Luke said, leaning slightly toward her.

"What?" she said. "Oh, yes, sure thing, Luke. You can come along to look at the accommodations if you like. But doesn't that sound just a tad boring to you?"

"Nooo," Luke said slowly, then smiled. "Not at all. Not even close."

Maggie narrowed her eyes. "Why not?"

Because he'd be envisioning the two of them in each of those suites, newly married, husband and wife, about to begin their honeymoon here in Phoenix before leaving on their dream trip. No, that didn't sound the least bit boring.

"Why not?" he said. Quick, St. John. Come up with something reasonable. "Because, like you, I've never seen a honeymoon suite in any of the ritzy hotels in town. It will be informative, interesting. Anytime a person has an opportunity to experience something new they should jump at the chance. It's good for the gray matter." He tapped his temple with a fingertip. "Know what I mean?"

"Not really," Maggie said, frowning, "but I'll take your word for it." She paused. "I think it would be best if I made actual appointments for our inspections. I'll get back to you on that."

"Fine. And you said you'd decided on the flowers for the wedding. What did you choose? No, wait, let me guess." Luke drummed the fingers of one hand on the table. "Hmm. You named your business Roses and Wishes. I'm betting that the bridal bouquet is roses, red for the holiday theme with some kind of Christmassy greens and those fluffy things that look sort of like snow."

"Baby's breath," Maggie said hardly above a whisper as she stared at Luke.

"Yeah, that's what it's called. How close did I come to being right?"

"That's exactly what I chose, but…but how did you know?"

Luke reached across the table and covered one of Maggie's hands with one of his. He gazed directly into her big brown eyes and when he spoke again his voice was slightly raspy and very, very…male. Maggie shivered.

"I knew because you're Maggie," he said. My Maggie. Forever.

"Oh," she said. Get your hand back, Maggie Jenkins. The heat—the heat from Luke's hand was traveling up her arm and across her breasts that were suddenly achy and… Get your dumb hand back. Sometime within the next hour. "Huh? You knew what flowers I'd pick right down to the baby's breath because I'm Maggie? I don't think that makes sense."

"It does to me," he said, tightening his grip slightly on her hand. "Yes, ma'am, it certainly does."

"Would you care for some dessert today?"

Maggie snatched her hand from beneath Luke's and looked up at the waitress.

"Dessert," she said, hearing the thread of breathlessness in her voice. "Dessert is a good thing. Yes, it certainly is, but I'm much too full to eat another bite of anything so…no, thank you."

Bingo, Luke thought. Maggie was flustered and that was dynamite. The heat that had rocketed throughout his body as he'd held her hand had traveled through her, too, he was certain of it. Her cheeks were flushed a delicate pink and her voice was trembling slightly. Fantastic.

"And you, sir?" the waitress said. "We have a scrumptious Black Forest cake today."

"A man certainly can't pass up Black Forest cake," Luke said. "Why don't you bring me a slice. With two forks, just in case the lady changes her mind and decides to share it with me."

"You bet," the waitress said. "I'll be right back."

A busboy cleared their dishes, and moments later the

waitress set an enormous slice of cake in the center of the table and placed a fork in front of Maggie, then Luke.

"Enjoy," the woman said, then zoomed away.

"Help yourself, Maggie," Luke said. "Look at that creation. Chocolate cake with whipped cream between the layers and all those cherries in sauce dribbling down the sides like a delicious waterfall. How can you resist a treat like this?"

What she wanted to know, Maggie thought miserably, was how could Luke make the description of a slab of cake sound like the most seductive thing she had ever heard in her entire life? The man just didn't quit.

"Well, maybe just one bite," she said, picking up the fork. She filled her fork, making sure it included one of the fat, gooey cherries. "Mmm."

"Oops," Luke said, reaching for a napkin. "You've got a dab of cherry sauce. I'll get it for you."

He leaned across the table and gently, so gently, dabbed at the spot of sauce, then shifted his eyes to look directly into Maggie's.

Her bones were dissolving, Maggie thought, unable to tear her gaze from Luke's. There was nothing sensuous about having her sloppy eating mopped up like a toddler in a high chair, darn it, but… Oh, yes, there was.

There was something so intimate about Luke tenderly stroking that napkin by her lips as though it was the most important thing he had ever done. She was going to slide off that chair and turn into a puddle on the floor.

"All better," he said, his voice husky. "Good cake?"

"Mmm," Maggie said dreamily. "The best cake I've ever…really yummy."

"Well, it's sure calling my name."

Maggie watched with rapt attention as Luke leveled a serving onto his fork, lifted it to his mouth, then closed his lips—those, oh-so-kissable lips—over the treat, then slowly pulled the fork free.

"Mmm," he said, closing his eyes as he savored the taste.

She couldn't handle this, Maggie thought frantically. She was going up in flames, burning inside with a heat like nothing she had ever experienced before.

Luke set the fork on the table and reached over to take both of Maggie's hands in his.

"Ah, Maggie," he said, "what are you doing to me? What is this thing that spins out of control between us?" It's love, Maggie Jenkins. True and forever love. "You feel it, I know you do."

"No, I don't," she said, trying to pull her hands free. Luke tightened his hold. "Well, yes, I do, but it's just physical attraction between two people who are…physically attracted to each other. I would call it lust, but that's kind of a tacky word. It's certainly nothing to be pursued or acted upon or… May I have my hands back now, please, Luke?"

"In a minute. So you admit that you're physically attracted to me?"

"Well…yes."

"You desire me? Do you, Maggie? Lust is a tacky word. Desire is something else entirely."

"Semantics."

"No, Maggie, emotions. Emotions are intertwined with desire. I truly believe that. The tricky part is to know what those emotions are, what they mean, unwrap them layer by layer like a wondrous gift."

"That's very poetic," Maggie said softly.

"I'm not attempting to be poetic. I'm just expressing how I feel. I want to know what that gift holds for us. Don't you?"

Maggie pulled her hands free and shook her head. "No, I can't."

"Why not?"

"Luke, you just don't understand."

"Then explain it to me. Please, Maggie. What are you afraid of? Why are you so determined to never marry, to plan weddings for so many brides but never one for yourself? Why have you built those tall, strong walls around your heart? There's something happening between us that could be very important, but whenever I bring it up you act like you're about to bolt. Talk to me. Please."

Maggie clutched her hands tightly in her lap and stared at them for a long, mind-searching moment. She nodded slowly, then met Luke's gaze again.

"All right," she said, her voice trembling slightly. "Perhaps I *should* tell you the truth about me, why none of the weddings I coordinate will ever be mine, why I'll never be a bride."

Luke's heart thudded so wildly he could hear the echo of it in his ears.

"It goes back as many generations as my family has been able to track, without skipping even one," Maggie continued. "There's no escaping it, no reason to believe it won't continue on and on into infinity." She sighed. "Oh, people try to beat the odds—my mother, sister, my brother—but it's foolish to do that because it's hopeless."

"My God, Maggie," Luke said, feeling the color drain from his face. "Is it a disease that can't be cured?"

"Well, I don't know if I'd call it a disease exactly, but there is definitely no cure for it. It happens over and over and over again. It's harsh and heartbreaking and I don't intend to allow it to happen to me. I will never, ever get married."

"What—" Luke cleared his throat "—what is it? Does it have an official name?"

"Yes, it definitely has a name," she said. "We're all doomed. It would be so foolish to believe I would be spared, because it wouldn't happen, Luke. My mother, sister, brother all thought they could escape from it, but…" She shook her head.

"What is it?" he said, leaning toward her. "You're ripping me up here, Maggie. *What is it?*"

Maggie took a shuddering breath, then blinked against sudden and unwelcome tears.

"It's…" she said, a sob catching in her throat. "It's the Jenkins Jinx."

Seven

It took several mental beats for Luke to really compute what Maggie had just said. He opened his mouth to reply, then shut it again as he replayed the words once more in his head.

The Jenkins Jinx? he thought incredulously. Did he have a clue as to what Maggie was talking about? No, he did not. A jinx of some kind that had a bearing on Maggie's negative attitude to marriage? Did people really believe in jinxes these days? A jinx that did what? Oh, man, this was nuts.

It would certainly clear things up if Maggie would suddenly laugh and tell him she was just kidding, that what she had said was a silly joke, then tell him the real reason she didn't intend to ever be the bride in one of her beautifully coordinated weddings.

But the fact that at the moment Maggie was a study in misery and that tears were shimmering in her big brown eyes told him that she was dead serious about the Jenkins Jinx.

"Maggie," Luke said finally, "we need to talk about this…this Jenkins Jinx thing, but you're obviously upset, so let's get out of here." He signaled to the waitress for the check. "I'll take you home, back to Roses and Wishes, and we'll discuss this there. Okay?"

"You said you had a very busy afternoon at work," Maggie said, then sniffled and dabbed her nose with the napkin.

"That's what cell phones are for," he said. "So bosses can call efficient secretaries and have them reschedule whatever is on the calendar. My father won't mind getting the word that he's free to go golfing."

"But I drove my van here so you can't take me home."

"I'll bring you back later for your van or you can drive yourself if you feel you're up to it," he said. "We're not postponing this discussion, Maggie."

Maggie sighed in defeat. "I had a feeling you'd say that. I'll drive myself. Meet me at Roses and Wishes." She got to her feet and hurried away.

Luke rose, dropped several bills onto the table, then accepted the check from the waitress.

"Is everything all right, sir?" the woman said.

"Ask me later," Luke said absently, "because right now I really don't know."

* * *

Maggie drove blindly to Roses and Wishes, wishing she could turn back the clock to before her momentous announcement about the Jenkins Jinx.

No, she thought with yet another sad-sounding sigh, there was no point in pretending the Jenkins Jinx didn't exist. Luke was pressing her to explore, actually embrace, the strange whatever-it-was that was happening between them, and it wasn't fair to keep the jinx a secret.

She dashed an errant tear from her cheek.

It just would have been nice, she mused wistfully, to have had more time with Luke, enjoy his company, allow herself to feel so feminine and desirable, before revealing the god-awful truth.

Once she explained it all to Luke, it would hover between them like a palpable entity, a living thing that would make him uncomfortable because she was a weird person from a very weird family.

"I'm so sad," Maggie said as she parked in front of Roses and Wishes. "So very, very sad."

She waited in the van until Luke arrived, then they entered the house together. Maggie left the Closed sign on the door.

"Let's go upstairs to the living room," she said, sounding extremely weary.

"Whatever you say," he said quietly.

In the tiny living room Maggie sank onto a rocking chair and Luke settled on the sofa, spreading his arms across the top as he looked at Maggie intently. She rocked back and forth for several minutes, staring into space.

"Maggie," Luke said, "you can't pretend I'm not sitting here waiting for you to talk to me."

She shifted her gaze to meet his.

"I know," she said. "It's just that I hate to… Never mind. You have the right to know what I meant by the Jenkins Jinx." She drew a steadying breath. "I told you that it goes back many generations in our family."

Luke nodded, aware that the lunch he'd consumed now felt like a rock in the pit of his stomach.

"We all have had to face the devastating fact," Maggie continued, "that for unknown reasons it is impossible for any of us to live happily ever after with our chosen mate. It just isn't going to happen, no matter what. And that, Luke, is the Jenkins Jinx."

Luke moved his arms forward to rest his elbows on his knees and make a steeple of his fingers.

"I beg your pardon?" he said, frowning.

"You heard me."

"Okay, I heard you, but I can't fathom that you actually believe that a jinx, a spell, whatever, has been cast over your entire family."

"Like a gloomy dark cloud," Maggie said, nodding.

"Maggie, come on, give me a break. Things like that don't really happen. So, yes, some of the couples in your clan got divorced, but—"

"Everyone got divorced."

"Everyone?" Luke said, raising his eyebrows.

"Everyone. We researched our family tree as far back as we could and, yes, everyone."

"That's rather…strange." Luke sank back against the cushions. "Whew."

"That's the Jenkins Jinx," Maggie said. "No one understands why we're plagued by it, what we did to draw this lousy card, but there's no denying the truth of it. Oh, there are those who feel they'll be the one to break the spell, end it for all time, because they're so in love, so sure when they marry that it's forever. Then—bam!— it all falls apart and yet another gleeful divorce attorney has a bill to send.

"My mother was a starry-eyed bride," she said. "My father left us when I was ten. Poof. Gone. My sister has been divorced twice, my brother once. My grandparents, great-grandparents… Oh, I can go even further back than that, I guarantee you. We all agree we're doomed."

"But—"

"Therefore, Luke, I never intend to fall in love and marry. I'm not going to have my dreams shattered and my heart broken. I'm not. So I create fairy-tale-perfect weddings for others to…to satisfy my romantic soul. But I'm beginning to wonder if Roses and Wishes is a dumb thing to be doing because it just emphasizes over and over what I'll never have."

"But you're planning the wedding of *your* dreams for Precious and Clyde," Luke said.

"Yes, and it's probably foolish, but I'm giving it to myself like a gift to cherish before I make a decision about whether I want to continue as a wedding coordinator."

Luke got to his feet and began to pace—as well as

he could in the limited space. He dragged a restless hand through his hair and narrowed his eyes in deep concentration. He finally stopped in front of Maggie's rocking chair, planted his hands on the arms and leaned down, speaking close to her lips as she stared at him in wide-eyed surprise.

"No," he said.

"No...what?" she said, aware, so very aware, that his lips were mere inches from hers.

"No, I won't accept this," he said. "So, okay, your family seems to have had more than your share of divorces, but there is no such thing as an honest-to-goodness jinx, Maggie."

"That's what my sister's second husband said—at first."

"Maggie, you're an intelligent woman," Luke said, his voice rising. "How can you buy into this malarkey?"

"Facts are facts," she said, matching his volume. "We checked as far back as we possibly could, hoping, praying, we'd find even one couple that stayed together on our family tree. There wasn't one. Not one, Luke. The jinx is real and I won't allow myself to think I could be the one to break it, make it disappear, because it's here to stay. That's the way it is and there's nothing I can do about it."

"It's impossible," he said none too quietly. "A jinx is a superstition, a...a... Damn it, this is the most frustrating conversation I've ever had in my entire life."

"Well, excuse me all the way to Sunday," Maggie yelled, "but the truth is the truth."

'Oh? Well, try this truth on for size, lady," Luke hollered.

He released his white-knuckle hold on the arms of the rocking chair, gripped Maggie's shoulders, hauled her to her feet…and kissed her.

Maggie stiffened in shock, but as Luke's kiss gentled and he dropped his hands from her shoulders to wrap his arms around her and bring her close to his body, she nestled against him. Her arms floated upward to encircle his neck, her fingertips inching into his thick ebony hair.

The kiss was hot. It was desire, not lust, with unnamed emotions intertwining with the want and need. The kiss was powerful enough to push aside for that tick of time the existence of the Jenkins Jinx and allow them to savor the taste, the feel, the very essence of each other. The kiss was theirs.

Luke broke away first to draw a much-needed breath but didn't release his hold on Maggie. She gazed up at him, a dreamy expression on her face, her lips moist and slightly parted, beckoning.

"Ah, Maggie," Luke said, his voice gritty with passion. "I want to make love with you so damn much. From the moment I first saw you I… Do you want me, Maggie? Do you want to make love with me?"

"Yes, I do," she whispered. "But—"

"Forget the jinx thing for now. We'll tackle that later…later…yes. All I can concentrate on now is you, me, what we'll share. But, Maggie, I would never take advantage of you, pressure you, attempt to seduce you into doing something you'll regret." He paused. "I guess what I'm saying is, it's your decision."

Oh, Maggie thought foggily. How could she decide when she couldn't even think clearly? Okay, okay, she was getting a grip now, ignoring the fact that she was still being held in Luke's strong arms, still molded to his aroused body, still...thinking. Yes, she was thinking.

And she wanted him.

She wanted to make love with him because she cared for him so very much and he cared for her, she knew he did.

And because when he realized that the Jenkins Jinx was true, he would chalk her up as being a very weird, creepy woman and keep her at a safe distance from him.

And because she intended to give herself this intimate joining with Luke St. John so she'd have a precious memory to make up for all she would never have because of the Jenkins Jinx.

"Maggie?"

"Make love with me, Luke," she said softly, looking directly into his dark eyes. "I won't be sorry. I'll have no regrets, I promise. We have no future together. None. The jinx is real and I've accepted that. Nothing you can say or do will change my mind about it. But now? Right now? I want—I desire you. So, please, make love with me."

With a groan that rumbled from deep in his chest, Luke captured Maggie's mouth once again in a searing kiss. She returned the kiss in total abandon, holding nothing back, giving as much as she was receiving.

Luke lifted his head, then swung Maggie up into his

arms. She pointed in the direction of her bedroom and he carried her there with long, purposeful strides.

He set her on her feet next to the double bed, absently registering that the room was femininity personified, just like Maggie, with a bedspread patterned with pale pink roses and a matching skirt on a small round table that held a clock and a telephone. The curtains were pink and the dresser was white wicker.

Maggie swept back the spread and blankets to reveal sheets with tiny pink rosebuds, then turned to face Luke again.

"I'm very nervous," she said. "I really don't have the kind of experience that I'm certain you're accustomed to and I—"

"Shh," he said, placing one fingertip gently on her lips. "We're going to be wonderful together, Maggie."

And they were.

With sudden confidence that came from a place she couldn't fathom, Maggie nodded, and as Luke shed his clothes, she removed her own. They stood naked before each other, rejoicing in what they saw, what would be theirs, given willingly.

He lifted her into his arms again, settled her in the center of the bed, then followed her down, his mouth melting over hers.

It was ecstasy. They kissed, caressed, discovered each other's mysteries with awe and wonder. Where hands traveled, lips followed, igniting the heat of their desire into leaping flames that threatened to consume them both.

Luke left her only long enough to roll on protection, then returned to her outstretched arms. When they could bear no more, he moved over her and into her with a thrust that filled her and brought a gasp of pure pleasure from her lips.

The rocking rhythm began, then increased in tempo until it was wild and earthy, wondrous, synchronized to perfection as though they had been lovers forever.

They soared. Higher. Closer. Calling to the other, clinging fast, then bursting upon the place they sought only seconds apart.

"Luke!"

"Oh, Maggie. My Maggie."

They drifted slowly back, then Luke mustered his last ounce of energy to move off her and tuck her close to his side, his lips resting lightly on her moist forehead. She rested one hand on the dark curls on his broad chest, feeling his heart settle into a quieter, steady beat.

"Thank you," Luke said quietly.

"And I thank *you*," Maggie whispered, "for the beautiful memories to keep."

Maggie's lashes drifted down and she slept, content, sated, a soft smile on her lips. Luke held her, sifting his fingers through her silky strawberry-blond curls.

God, how he loved this woman, he thought, feeling a foreign ache tighten his throat. She had given of herself so freely, so honestly, to him. *Him.* She cared deeply for him, he knew that, might even be falling in love with him just as he was already deeply in love with her.

He couldn't lose her. No, the mere thought of it was

more than he could bear. He knew the name of the enemy now—the Jenkins Jinx. That he believed it to be crazy, borderline nuts, meant nothing because Maggie was convinced it was true and planned to never marry to protect her heart from being shattered.

The battle lines were drawn. He was literally fighting for his life, his future happiness, his forever. And he would be the victor, for himself, for Maggie, for what they would have together until death parted them and beyond.

He would win. Somehow. He had to.

"I love you, Maggie Jenkins," he whispered, tightening his hold on her. "You are my life. My wife. Mine."

A little over an hour later Maggie stirred and opened her eyes, only to blink against the bright sunlight streaming through the window.

Luke, she thought, as the mist of sleep lifted.

She turned her head on the pillow to see the empty expanse of bed next to her, then heard the sound of the shower running. She stretched leisurely, then pulled the sheet to beneath her chin, clutching it with both hands.

She'd made love with Luke, she thought, and it had been glorious, beyond her wildest fantasies. Did she regret what she had done? Was she sorry? No. Never.

Her life was not like other women's, with dreams of a husband, babies, hearth and home. To have experienced something as wondrous as she just had with a magnificent man like Luke St. John was more than she'd ever expected to receive, to possess as hers, to tuck away in the treasure chest in her heart.

Was this dangerous? she asked herself. Well, no, not if she stayed alert, kept a tight control over her emotions and the truth of her reality front and center. She could handle this. She would have this time with Luke. And when Precious and Clyde were married, that would be the end of Maggie Jenkins and Luke St. John. She knew that, understood that. Yes, she could handle this.

Luke came into the bedroom fully dressed, his hair damp from the shower. He sat on the edge of the bed and smiled at Maggie.

"Have a nice nap?"

"Lovely, thank you," she said, matching his smile.

"You're very pretty when you're sleeping, very peaceful." He paused. "I'd better get going. You'll let me know when you have some appointments to see honeymoon suites at various hotels?"

"Yes, of course. I'll call you."

"Good." He nodded. "Maggie, you don't have any regrets about what happened here, do you?"

"No, no, Luke, not at all. It was wonderful and I… No regrets. We both understand that this is temporary, what we're sharing, because my life is what it is— jinxed. I know you're not quite believing that yet, but it's true, trust me, and I'll never allow myself to think otherwise. That would be so foolish on my part and it isn't going to happen."

"Mmm." Luke frowned. "And no one in the entire history of your family has figured out a way to break the spell, the jinx?"

"No."

"Mmm." Luke stroked his chin thoughtfully. "Would you categorize the jinx as a superstition of sorts?"

"I… Well, not exactly, because it's true."

"But if you had to group it with something," he said, "a jinx would fall into the arena of superstitions for a lack of a better place to put it. Right?"

"I suppose so. I never thought about it like that." Maggie looked at him questioningly. "Why?"

"I'm just trying to be certain that I fully understand the Jenkins Jinx, what it is."

"It's my reality," Maggie said firmly. "Ask any member of my family and they'll verify what I'm saying. It's sad but true."

"Yeah." Luke leaned over and dropped a quick kiss on Maggie's lips. "I'll be waiting to hear from you about viewing the suites. Eager to hear from you. You'll contact me soon?"

"Yes, sir," she said, smiling at him warmly.

Luke drew one thumb lightly over her lips, which she felt to the very tip of her toes, then he got to his feet and left the room.

"'Bye," Maggie whispered, then sighed in delicious contentment.

After a frustrating stop-and-start drive across town in the surging Phoenix traffic Luke entered the plush offices of St. John and St. John, Attorneys at Law.

"Good afternoon, Mr. St. John," the receptionist said.

"Mmm," Luke said absently as he strode down the hall.

The attractive young woman turned in her chair and

watched him go, deciding he was definitely a man with something heavy on his mind.

Luke stopped at the desk of his secretary, a plump woman in her fifties, who looked up at him with a rather confused expression.

"I thought you said when you called that you weren't coming in this afternoon," she said.

"I need some data, Betty," he said. "Extensive research."

Betty picked up a pen and slid a steno pad in front of her.

"Okay," she said. "What can I do for you, Luke? What am I researching?"

"Superstitions."

"I beg your pardon? Superstitions? About what? Is this pertaining to a case you have on the docket?"

"Not exactly," he said, shoving his hands into his pockets. "Let's just say it's the most important project I've ever undertaken and let it go at that, shall we? Start with superstitions regarding brides, weddings, things like that, then go further into superstitions in general."

"Brides? You mean, like it's bad luck for the groom to see the bride in her wedding dress before she walks down the aisle?"

"Exactly." He shook his head. "Who comes up with this junk?"

Betty shrugged. "I have no idea, but that business about the dress has been around for as long as I can remember, and I'm borderline ancient." She tapped the pen against the pad of paper. "Okay. I get the drift of what you want about brides and what have you. Then I go to other things like not walking under a ladder or letting a black cat cross your path?"

"Right."

"When do you need this interesting info?"

"Yesterday," he said, then went on into his office.

Late that night Luke was stretched out on the sofa in his living room reading yet again the thick stack of papers that Betty had given him on superstitions.

He frowned in disbelief at some of them and couldn't help but laugh aloud at others. But for the most part he was digesting everything he read with serious intent.

He'd memorize as many of these wacky things as he could, he'd decided, then keep the papers close at hand for ready reference on others.

Luke reached over and set the papers on the coffee table fronting the sofa, then laced his fingers beneath his head where it rested on a puffy throw pillow.

The Plan was in effect, he mused, insofar as Maggie believed she was coordinating a wedding for cousin Clyde and his Precious.

However, now he knew Maggie's secret about the Jenkins Jinx, further genius-level action was definitely called for, an extension of The Plan. Through brilliant lawyer-type persuasion he'd gotten Maggie to agree that the jinx was a superstition. She'd done so rather reluctantly, but he'd take what he could get.

His mission, then, was to cleverly and carefully expose Maggie to superstition after superstition, casually pointing out that, son of a gun, nothing horrible had happened because they'd—they'd what?—walked under a ladder, for example. He'd stack up the evidence piece by piece, inching closer and closer to the Jenkins Jinx and the miraculous fact that Maggie was obviously the one who was going to break its hold on the family because she was immune to the consequences of superstitions.

Man, he was so sharp sometimes, it just blew his mind. This was shining-star thinking, damn it. It wouldn't be easy, that was for sure, would take planning and coordination and… He needed help. It was too big, too important to tackle alone.

Luke sat up and swung his feet to the floor.

His father, he thought. Mason St. John knew about The Plan and understood the need for it, although he did have some reservations about the consequences of duping Maggie. His dad was the perfect person to help with this new addition to the program.

Luke glanced at his watch and swore under his breath as he saw it was too late to call his father.

But first thing in the morning, he thought, he'd corner his dad and they'd map things out. Ah, yeah, this was good, very good. It was the next step in the battle that would eventually win the war.

Luke settled back on the sofa and smiled up at the ceiling.

Yes, there was going to be a Christmas wedding, all right. But Precious and Clyde—who were becoming strangely real to him—would have to make their own arrangements to tie the knot.

The wedding that was being put together at this very moment would unite Maggie Jenkins and Luke St. John in holy matrimony forever, declare them to be wife and husband, soul mates, partners in life and parents of the little miracles that would be the result of their exquisite lovemaking.

His Christmas bride, Luke thought. His Maggie.

Eight

Maggie spent the next two days tackling the stack of paperwork in her office at Roses and Wishes. It was her least favorite part of owning the business, and she often daydreamed about what it would be like to be successful enough to have a secretary.

Not only would the tedious paperwork be taken care of, but Roses and Wishes could remain open while Maggie was off and running to tend to the multitude of details, details, details needed to coordinate the perfect wedding.

But, she mused as she scrutinized another bill for Ginger and Robert's extravaganza, the budget didn't allow for such luxury as a secretary. And besides, she wasn't all that sure she intended to continue with this career choice she'd been so excited about at the onset.

Maggie sighed and read the bill once more, realizing that yet again she hadn't comprehended what was on the invoice. Why? Because her mind kept drifting off and settling on the exquisite lovemaking she'd enjoyed with Luke.

She should have had her desk cleared in one day but, no, not this time. Here it was late in the afternoon of the second day and she was still glued to her chair because her flighty brain wouldn't behave itself.

Maggie flipped the paper in the air, watched it settle on the pile she had yet to even look at, then plunked her elbow on the desktop and rested her chin in her palm.

All right, she thought decisively, this obviously wasn't working well. Sneaky and wonderful images of that afternoon with Luke kept creeping in and disrupting her concentration. So, therefore, she'd indulge in a trip down memory lane, relive every tantalizing, sensuous moment of what they'd shared and finally put it to rest. Then she'd be able to get her chores done like a proper little business owner should.

Maggie stared into space, making no attempt to erase the soft smile that formed on her lips as picture after picture slid into her mind and sensation after sensation swirled within her body.

Heat settled low within her, pulsing and hot, and she shifted slightly on the chair. Her breasts began to ache, yearning for the soothing feeling of Luke's hands, then mouth, on the sensitive flesh. Mercy. Her cheeks, she knew, were flushed and she could hear the increased tempo of her heart echoing in her ears.

Ecstasy in its purest form, she mused dreamily. That's what that joining had been. And at the peak of it, the climax? God, she had no idea it could be like that. It defied description, required words that hadn't even been invented yet.

Imagine what it would be like, she mentally rambled on, to be married to Luke, to be the recipient of all that magnificent masculinity night after night after… It boggled the mind.

Of course, there was more to marriage than just…well, than just that. She and Luke would laugh and talk, eat meals together, shop for groceries, discuss events from the six-o'clock news. They'd choose a house they both knew would be their home, then furnish it room by room, agreeing on choices, compromising where necessary.

And, of course, one of those rooms would be a nursery for the baby they'd create with their wondrous love-making. A baby boy? A girl? It wouldn't matter. Then a couple of years later another little miracle would arrive to join the first. Luke would be a fantastic father to all their children, whether they had two or four or…

But each night when tiny heads were nestled on pillows after stories had been read and prayers heard, it would be grown-up time, Maggie-and-Luke time, private time. And in their marriage bed they would reach eagerly for each other, the desire never waning, their heartfelt love growing deeper and stronger with each passing year. Their lips would meet and…

"Maggie?"

Maggie shifted her gaze to focus on the direction the voice had come from. Luke. He was standing right in front of her desk in all his masculine splendor.

He really wasn't there, she told herself, was a figment of her imagination due to the fantasy playing out in her head. No, he really wasn't there, so what the heck....

Maggie got to her feet, leaned forward to grip Luke's tie and pulled him toward her to plant a searing kiss on his lips.

But the very moment that their mouths met, a mortified Maggie realized that Luke really *was* there in living, breathing color. She released her hold on his tie and plunked back down in her chair, wishing she could disappear into thin air, never to be seen again.

"Well," Luke said, smoothing his tie and smiling at her, "that was quite a welcome. Hello to you, too, Maggie."

"'Lo," she mumbled, staring at the middle button on his shirt.

"You certainly make a man feel special, like you're glad to see him, I must say."

"I can explain that," Maggie said, finally meeting his gaze. She sighed and shook her head. "No, forget it. It's too ridiculous." She paused. "I guess you're here because you haven't heard from me regarding honeymoon suites, but I've been buried in paperwork and haven't had a chance to do any investigating yet."

"No, I'm here because I missed you," Luke said, settling onto one of the chairs opposite Maggie's desk. "That's it, pure and simple."

"Really?" A bright smile lit up Maggie's face, then

in the next instant she managed to erase it and adopt an expression of vague interest. "Oh?"

"Yep," Luke said, chuckling. "And since this tie I'm wearing may never be the same, I'd say you missed me, too."

"Well..." Maggie flipped one hand in the air. "Whatever."

"Mmm. My, my, Maggie, I'm surprised to see that you're wearing that shade of blue on a Thursday. You didn't go so far as to take a bath or shower this morning, did you?"

"Huh?" Maggie peered down at the string sweater she wore, then looked at Luke again, obviously confused. "What on earth are you talking about?"

Luke propped his elbows on the arms of the chair and tented his fingers.

"There are certain cultures," he said, "which believe the color blue represents the ocean, the sea. They also think that Thursday is the unluckiest day of the week. Therefore, to tempt fate by wearing that color on a Thursday, you're destined to have an accident in water, maybe even drown."

"That's the silliest thing I've ever heard," Maggie said, rolling her eyes heavenward.

"Not to the people who believe it."

"Which probably number about three. For heaven's sake, Luke, the wrong color on the wrong day and you're deader than a doornail? That's a nonsense-to-the-max superstition."

Luke shrugged with a rather nondescript expression on his face.

"Besides, I took a long bath in my wonderful tub this morning and lived to tell about it," she said, lifting her chin. "So there."

"No kidding? Well, maybe that superstition is garbage after all," he said thoughtfully. "It was so off-the-wall that I was leaning toward believing it. I mean, there must be enough evidence to substantiate it in the first place."

Maggie leaned toward him. "That tie of yours that I just wrinkled is blue, sort of sea-blue. Did you shower this morning?"

"Yes, I did."

"I rest my case. That superstition is nonsense."

Gotcha, Luke thought smugly. Score one for Luke St. John.

"So back to why you're here," Maggie said.

"Well, it's not because I'm bugging you about the honeymoon suites," Luke said. "One of my clients had a bit of an emergency and I had to put on my big-boy-lawyer clothes and meet with him for a long, boring lunch close to here. I just dropped in to say hello and to tell you that I missed you." He attempted once again to smooth his crumpled tie. "And to get my tie killed, I guess."

"I'd offer to replace it, but I don't think I could afford to do that on my budget. How much did it cost?"

"A hundred and fifty dollars."

"For a tie?" she said, nearly shrieking. "That's absurd."

"It's imported silk from Italy."

"Could I interest you in installment payments?"

Luke laughed. "Tell you what. You agree to have dinner with me tonight and we'll call it even."

"Well…"

"I'm in the mood for pizza, if that suits you, so dress very casually. But don't wear blue. Okay?"

"Pizza sounds great but, Luke, you've got to forget about that superstition because it really is nuts."

"I'll try," he said, rising with a dramatic sigh. "I'll pick you up at eight o'clock. I'll let you get back to work now. See you later."

"But…" Maggie said as Luke strode from the room. She smiled as she heard the front door of Roses and Wishes close behind him. "Eight o'clock will be just fine."

She picked up an invoice, then stared into space.

She'd really gotten carried away with her mental fantasy, she mused. Goodness, she'd gone all the way to being Luke's wife and having a slew of his babies. Well, that was all right…except, of course, for the embarrassing tie episode.

It didn't matter how much daydreaming she did because she knew, really knew, that all this was temporary. She could indulge in anything she wanted to with Luke St. John because once Precious and Clyde were married that would be that. No more Luke in her life. In the meantime? She was free to go for it because she had total command over her emotions. Everything was dandy.

That night Luke drove past several well-known pizza restaurants to the far side of Phoenix.

"You must really like the pizza here," Maggie said,

as they settled into a red vinyl booth. "You certainly were willing to drive a long way to reach this place."

"Best pizza in Phoenix," Luke said, glancing at his watch. "I'll go up and place our order. What would you like on yours?"

"Anything and everything except the little fishes," she said, smiling.

"Got it," he said, sliding out of the booth. "Soda?"

"Perfect."

A few minutes later Luke returned to sit across from Maggie and set a slip of paper on the table.

"I'm glad this is Thursday and not Friday," he said. "We have the number thirteen. Thirteen on a Friday is bad news, you know." He looked at his watch again.

"No worse than drowning in the bathtub because you wore the wrong color," Maggie said drily. "Luke, what is with this sudden preoccupation with superstitions?"

"It's not sudden," he said. Oh, man, his nose was going to grow. "I've always been superstitious, but don't talk about it much because people have a tendency to scoff."

"Scoff?"

"Yes, definitely scoff. But, you see, Maggie, I've been doing a great deal of thinking about what you told me about the Jenkins Jinx. My first reaction was to tell you that it was nonsense. I scoffed. And I apologize to you for doing that. Jinxes, superstitions, wives' tales all have merit. I want you to know that I respect your belief in the Jenkins Jinx."

"You do? I mean, you're not going to attempt to talk

me out of it? Tell me it's a bunch of baloney? Try to convince me that I could be a bride, get married, just like anyone else?"

"Nope."

"Oh."

Well, that was good, she thought. Wasn't it? Sure. Then why did she suddenly feel so sad, gloomy and depressed? Luke's acceptance of the Jenkins Jinx meant he was as fully prepared to walk away as she was after Precious and Clyde's wedding. No fuss, no muss. That was…great. But her stomach hurt. And her heart hurt. Her heart actually hurt. Damn it, what was the matter with her?

"Luke, my boy," a deep voice boomed, snapping Maggie back to attention.

"Well, Dad, my, my, what are you doing here?" Luke said, looking up at his father where he stood next to the table.

"Your mother got hungry for pizza so I called in an order and came to pick it up. This place has the best pizza in Phoenix, you know."

"Yes, I certainly know that and you're fortunate to live only a few blocks away," Luke said. "You remember Maggie."

"Certainly," Mason St. John said. "Delightful to see you again, my dear."

"My pleasure," Maggie said.

"Luke, I'm just beside myself," Mason said.

"Oh? Why is that, pray tell?" Luke said.

Pray tell? Maggie thought. For some dumb reason

Luke and his father sounded like they were reading words from a script and not doing a very good job of it. No, that was silly. So what, pray tell, was Mr. St. John beside himself about?

"I lost my acorn," Mason said.

Huh? Maggie thought, frowning slightly.

"Oh, no, anything but that, Father."

"I know, I know," Mason said, resting one hand on his heart. "I didn't tell your mother I was driving over here without my acorn. She'd be worried sick."

"For good reason," Luke said. "But fear not, because I always carry two." He leaned back so he could slide his hand into the front pocket of his jeans. "There you go, sir. One acorn."

Mason curled his fingers around the acorn Luke had placed in his hand, then slid the little nut into his pocket. He clamped one hand on Luke's shoulder.

"Bless you, son. Enjoy your pizza. Good night, Maggie. Farewell, Luke."

As Mason hurried away, the waitress appeared at the table and set a pitcher of soda in the center along with two glasses. Luke thanked the young girl, then filled the glasses. Maggie leaned forward, staring at Luke intently as she waited for an explanation about the bizarre interchange regarding the acorn. Luke glanced around.

"Sure is getting crowded in here, isn't it? That's understandable, though, when you consider that they serve—"

"The best pizza in Phoenix," Maggie finished for him. "Would you care to explain what just happened here?"

"The waitress delivered our soda," Luke said, smiling. "Hey, they just called number eleven. We're getting closer. Man, I'm starved."

"Luke," Maggie said, smacking the table with the palm of her hand. Luke cringed. "What was that whole weird thing with your father about the acorn?"

"Oh, *that*," Luke said. "Did they just call number twelve?"

"Luke," Maggie said, narrowing her eyes and drumming the fingers of one hand on the top of the table. "The acorn. Now."

"You bet," he said, nodding. "Well, it's very simple. It's good luck to carry an acorn on one's person. We St. Johns have toted acorns around for years. Years and years. Never go anywhere without our acorns, by golly. So you can see why my father was so upset about having lost his and not wishing my poor mother to know. But—" he grinned "—I saved his bacon because I always have two. Insurance, you know what I mean?"

Maggie leaned back in the booth and crossed her arms over her chest. "That's stupid," she said.

"It certainly is not," Luke said indignantly. "One could become jinxed, experience endless lousy luck if one didn't carry one's acorn, Maggie. Remind me to find an acorn for you." He paused. "Yo. They just called thirteen. That's us. I'll be back in a flash."

"But…" Maggie said, pointing one finger in the air, then realizing that Luke was long gone.

All the St. Johns were superstition freaks? she thought incredulously. They were intelligent, highly educated people, lawyers and what have you, for heaven's sake, but they flipped out if they lost their acorn? How weird was that?

Luke interrupted Maggie's racing thoughts by setting a huge, fragrant pizza in the center of the table, then sitting down again and rubbing his hands together.

"Now that looks delicious," he said, smiling. "Dig in and enjoy."

"I will, but…Luke, about this acorn thing. Your father didn't say he'd experienced any bad luck or mishaps or whatever while his acorn was missing. Correct?"

Luke nodded as he chewed a big bite of the hot pizza.

"So," Maggie continued, "doesn't that suggest that there is nothing to the superstition surrounding the acorn? That it is just that—a superstition, which is fun and cute but…isn't grounded in reality?"

Luke stared into space. "You've got a point there. When I was a kid I left my acorn in the pocket of my jeans and my mom washed them, turned the acorn into a mushy mess. It was quite a while before I could find another one because it was the wrong time of year. Nothing bad happened to me except that I flunked a spelling test, which was my fault because I didn't study for it."

Maggie picked up a slice of pizza and smiled, obviously pleased with herself. "See?" She took a bite of her dinner.

"I'll give this some serious thought," Luke said. Oh, this was going great, even better than he had hoped for. "Wait a minute here."

"Hmm?" Maggie said, her mouth full of pizza.

"I bet you didn't know that if you say goodbye to a friend on a bridge you'll never see each other again. Well, when I was fifteen I had this buddy. We did everything together, were really close. One summer we were riding our bikes and said goodbye at the end of the day on a bridge. I never saw him again. How do you like that?"

"Why didn't you ever see him again?" Maggie said.

"Because of the bridge thing, Maggie." Luke paused. "Well, not entirely, I guess. His dad was a creep, physically abused his mom and... She took off in the middle of the night with my buddy and disappeared.

"I figured it was because of the parting on the bridge, but now that I really think about it... Well, hell, so much for the bridge belief." He shook his head. "Amazing. All these years I was convinced...mmm."

Maggie smiled sweetly. "This pizza is delicious. Thank you for bringing me here."

"Sure, no problem," Luke said, frowning. "This is rather unsettling. The acorn. The bridge. I don't really have any concrete data to... Just goes to show ya, doesn't it? Things aren't always what they seem to be. Ready for some more soda?"

"No, I'm fine," Maggie said. "Don't be so hard on yourself, Luke. You got caught up in the theories about the acorn and the bridge, have believed them for so long you haven't questioned their validity in years. I think you're being very noble—there's a good word—to accept that the superstitions about them aren't real, aren't true."

"You're right," he said, "and I have you to thank for

showing me how ridiculous I was for buying into those tales." He deserved an Academy Award for this performance, he really did. "Let's just concentrate on the pizza now. This has been a pretty heavy topic for my weary brain. Enough for one night."

"Okay. Do you want to discuss Precious and Clyde's wedding?"

Luke smiled. "Maggie, I'd love to discuss the wedding. You have no idea how much it means to me."

"Well, the church is reserved for December twenty-third," Maggie said, her voice ringing with excitement. "And I got the ballroom at the Majestic Palms Hotel sewn up for the reception."

"The Majestic Palms," Luke said, nodding in approval. "Classy. Very nice."

"I have an appointment next week to meet with the chef to plan the buffet dinner at the reception. I still have oodles to do—you know, decide on the color of the tablecloths, the centerpieces, start shopping around for the exact shade of material I want for the bridesmaids' dresses and, of course, there's the wedding dress itself."

"Yep."

"What about the invitations, Luke? Do you think Precious and Clyde would prefer traditional ones that say the name of the parents or a more modern version where the couple themselves are inviting everyone to share their special event?"

Uh-oh, Luke thought, then took a big bite of pizza to give himself time to consider his answer. The invitations couldn't be ordered with Precious and Clyde's names on them. They didn't even exist. Think, St. John.

"Um…why don't you hold off on the invitations for now," he said finally. "I should run that by Precious and Clyde just in case they have an idea as to what will make the mothers happy."

"Okay. Would you ask them how they feel about tiny holly berries edging the invitations? I thought that would be so festive for a Christmas wedding."

"I'm sure that part will be fine. There certainly are a lot of things to tend to for a picture-perfect wedding, aren't there?"

"It takes months," Maggie said, laughing, "and then—blink—the ceremony is over in about fifteen minutes." She frowned in the next instant. "And in our family the marriage lasts about that long, too."

Change the subject, Luke thought frantically. He didn't want Maggie centering on the Jenkins Jinx, not tonight. Her beautiful eyes sparkled when she talked about the plans for the wedding, and the expression on her face was pure joy.

Not only that, he needed more superstitions for her to dismiss, to attempt to talk him out of believing, if he was to build a solid foundation for his case.

No, the Jenkins Jinx was definitely off-limits this evening.

"You know," he said, "you've never seen my apartment. I was just thinking that I have some mint-chocolate-chip ice cream in my freezer. Would you like to go there for dessert?"

Maggie leaned toward him. "Mint-chocolate-chip?"

"That's the one."

"Two scoops?"

"Three scoops," he said, holding up that many fingers.

"I have no willpower when it comes to mint-chocolate-chip ice cream," Maggie said. "Oh, my, three scoops."

"I thought you might like that flavor," Luke said, appearing extremely pleased with himself. "See how well I'm getting to know you, Maggie? It boggles the mind."

It terrifies the mind, Maggie thought. They were becoming so connected, bonded, on the same wavelength and... Never mind. She wasn't going to get all in a dither about it.

She was about to have three scoops of mint-chocolate-chip ice cream. Ah, yes, life was good.

Nine

"**M**y goodness," Maggie said, taking in Luke's enormous living room. "This is incredible, just beautiful. I've never been in a penthouse apartment before. The view is fabulous. I'd probably lose track of time and just sit for hours gazing out those windows at the city lights. You must look forward to coming home each day after work, Luke."

Not anymore, Luke thought as he stared at the awed expression on Maggie's face. Now it was just a whole lot of empty space waiting for Maggie to fill it to overflowing with her sunshine, laughter and…well, by just being Maggie.

"Ready for that ice cream?" he said.

"Sure. Can I see the kitchen?"

Luke laughed. "Follow me. It's fun to experience this place through fresh eyes."

Maggie gushed on and on about the fantastic kitchen as Luke scooped out the ice cream. As he picked up the bowls to carry them to the table, he dropped one of the spoons.

"Darn," he said.

"I'll get it," Maggie said, retrieving the spoon from the floor and rinsing it under the faucet.

They settled onto chairs opposite each other at the round oak table and Maggie took several mouthfuls of the dessert before she realized that Luke was staring into space.

"What's wrong?" she said.

"I was just wondering what child was going to come visit me and I'm coming up blank."

"I beg your pardon?" Maggie said, obviously confused.

"When you drop a spoon it means a child will visit. A fork brings a woman to your door, and a knife indicates the visitor will be a man."

"Is that a fact," Maggie said drily.

"Yep."

"Mmm," Maggie said, frowning at him.

"It's true," Luke said, leaning toward her. "I dropped a knife last month and—bingo—Robert popped in for no reason other than he was in the neighborhood."

"Robert is your brother. It makes perfect sense that he'd like to see you. It has nothing to do with the knife you dropped, Luke."

"Oh, yeah? Well, another time it was a fork, and

you'd better believe I shoved all the dirty dishes in the dishwasher before the knock came at the door. And there she was, my mother, bringing me some brownies she'd baked." He paused. "I wonder what little kid... Are Girl Scouts selling cookies now or something?"

"Halt," Maggie said, raising one hand. "Has Robert ever come by unannounced before?"

"Well...yes."

"And is your mother in the habit of bringing you homemade baked goods?"

"Yes, but—"

"I rest my case. Your fumble-fingers with the silverware was just a coincidence, nothing more. Another one of those superstitions you should forget about."

"Think so?"

"Know so." Maggie took another spoonful of ice cream. "Mmm. This is delicious. You'd better start on yours before it melts."

"You're really punching holes in my superstitions, you know," Luke said, then started in on his dessert.

"They can control your life if you're not careful," Maggie said.

Luke laughed. "Not all of them. There's one just for women. If she goes out in public and her slip shows, it means her father loves her more than her mother does."

"No, Luke, it means that either her slip is too long or her dress is too short."

"What you're saying makes sense, I guess. Then again...hmm. I'll have to think about this." He paused.

"Enough about superstitions. I'm going to go put some music on. I'll be right back."

A few moments later Maggie stiffened in her chair as the sound of lilting music reached her.

Oh, God, she thought, that was one of the waltzes she and Luke had danced to at Ginger and Robert's wedding. The beautiful song evoked special memories she intended to keep for all time. Did Luke remember why that particular tune was so meaningful or was it just a coincidence that he had put it on? No, men didn't get caught up in things like that. Music was music.

Luke came back into the kitchen and stood next to Maggie's chair.

"Recognize that waltz?" he said quietly. "We danced to it at Robert and Ginger's wedding. I asked the band leader what it was and went out and bought it so I could play it when you came here."

"Really?" Maggie said, a warmth suffusing her and creating a flush on her cheeks. "You did that? Of course I remember it, Luke, but to think that you went to all this trouble to… I don't know what to say."

He extended one hand toward her. "Say you'll dance with me."

From a seemingly faraway dreamy place, Maggie watched her hand float up to grasp Luke's, then she was on her feet and in his embrace. He held her close, moving with the music as he glided them out of the kitchen and into the living room, which was filled with the melody from speakers mounted high on the wall in each corner of the large room.

Maggie nestled her head on Luke's shoulder as they danced, drinking in the feel of him, his aroma, the strength of his body. Around the room they went, so gracefully, so perfectly in step.

It was so romantic that tears burned at the back of Maggie's eyes and desire consumed her, making it impossible to think clearly. She could only feel and savor and wish for the music to never end.

But it did finish, and they stopped in front of the tall windows where the lights of the city spread out in all directions like a fairyland. Another song started, but they didn't move, just held fast to each other. Then Luke shifted enough so he could tilt Maggie's chin up with one gentle fingertip, lowered his head and kissed her.

The kiss was so soft and tender, so exactly right to mark the finish of the memory-filled waltz, that two tears spilled onto Maggie's cheeks. Luke deepened the kiss and she gave herself to him, swept away by the moment and the music and…Luke.

Then he slowly, so slowly, lowered her to the plush carpet. He stretched out next to her, bracing his weight on one forearm as he drew a thumb over her tears.

"You're so beautiful," he said, his voice husky. "I've actually daydreamed about this, about seeing you here in my home, right here in front of these windows with the world spread out before us as though it belongs only to us. Ah, Maggie, I…" *Love you with all that I am, all I will ever be, for eternity.* "I…want to make love to you so much, so very much."

"Yes," she whispered.

He kissed her, then they parted long enough to shed their clothes and reached for each other once again. An urgency engulfed them, a need so great it was indescribable.

With hands never still, they caressed.

With lips seeking more, they kissed.

With passion soaring to unbelievable heights, they waited until they could bear it no longer.

Then they joined, meshed into one entity that made it impossible to decipher where the body soft and feminine and the one so very masculine ended and began.

The music had stopped, but they could hear their special waltz as they rocked in gentle rhythm to the exquisite song that belonged to them alone. The tension built within them, tightening, spiraling, taking them higher, up and away, until they burst into the heavens with the lights of their world beyond the windows showing them the way.

It was ecstasy. It was nearly shattering in its splendor, an explosion of sensations like none before. They drifted, savoring, murmuring the name of the other, until they returned to rest on the lush carpet that cradled them.

Luke moved off Maggie, then shifted her so her back was to his front and they could gaze out at the lights. He buried his face in her fragrant hair for a long moment, then tucked her head beneath his chin.

Maggie drew a shuddering breath, then smothered a sob that threatened to escape from her throat.

Dear God, she thought, she loved him. She was in love with Luke St. John. There was no denying it, nowhere to hide from the truth of it, nowhere to run. She loved him. He was all, everything and more that she'd fantasized about finding in a man, the one who would steal her heart for all time if things were different. If she was a normal woman, not plagued by the Jenkins Jinx. She loved him, but she couldn't have him, and it was just so incredibly sad.

But for now? she thought, blinking back unwelcomed tears. He was hers. Until Precious and Clyde's wedding, Luke was hers. She would cherish every moment she had with him and ignore the ticking of the clock that would signal their goodbye.

"What we just shared was…" Luke said, then stopped speaking for a second. "No, I don't have the words."

"I don't either," Maggie said softly, "but I know that it was… I'll never forget this night, Luke."

"I won't either." He paused, then chuckled. "I think our ice cream has melted."

Maggie smiled. "I think my bones have melted."

Time lost meaning as they lay together in sated, comfortable silence, then Maggie finally sighed.

"I'm about to fall asleep," she said. "I'd better get home, Luke."

"Ah, Maggie, stay. Please," he said. "We'll sleep with our heads on the same pillow in my bed and have breakfast together in the morning."

"I don't think…"

"Please?"

Why not? Maggie thought. In for a penny, in for a pound, or however that saying went. She was hopelessly, irrevocably in love with this man. The damage was done, the heartbreak guaranteed when all of this ended. Why not share everything she could with Luke while it was possible?

"Yes," she said. "Yes, I'll stay."

"Thank you," Luke said, then shifted away from her, rolled to his feet and extended one hand to her. "Come on. I promise my bed is softer than this floor."

Maggie placed her hand in his and allowed him to draw her up into an embrace where his mouth melted over hers in a searing kiss. On legs that weren't quite steady she walked by his side to the large master bedroom that was decorated in gray and burgundy. Luke turned on a lamp on the nightstand, then flipped back the blankets to reveal burgundy sheets.

"Oh, wait," he said. "Make note of which side of the bed you get in on because you have to leave on the same side in the morning or you'll have bad luck."

"Here we go again," Maggie said, rolling her eyes. "Another St. John superstition."

"Well," he said, shrugging, "at least I have a variety to offer. You're zoned in on the Jenkins Jinx and that's it."

Maggie looked up at him and frowned. "Which has generations of proof that validates it."

"That may be true, but you've managed to punch holes in all the superstitions I've presented so far, shown me that there's room for doubt. The same may hold true for your jinx."

"No," Maggie said, taking a step backward. "I'm not going to even entertain the idea that the jinx can be broken. I've seen the heartache suffered by those who thought they could do exactly that. No."

"Okay," Luke said, raising both hands in a gesture of peace. "Forget I said that. I didn't mean to upset you on this incredibly perfect night." He swept one arm in the direction of the bed. "Madam?"

Maggie settled onto the bed with a sigh of pleasure.

"Oh, this is heavenly," she said.

"I'm going to go turn out the lights in the other rooms and dump the soupy ice cream," Luke said. "I'll be back in a few minutes."

"'Kay," she said, then yawned.

Luke chuckled, then strode from the room. When he returned, Maggie was sound asleep. He slipped carefully into the bed next to her, then propped up on one forearm to watch her sleep.

So lovely, he thought. Maggie was here with him, where she belonged. If only there was a golden ring on her finger symbolizing her being his wife, his partner in life.

He was winning little victories each time she made it clear that the newest superstition he'd declared was foolish, should be dismissed as nonsense. Each of those incidents gave him ammunition to demolish the Jenkins Jinx. He was definitely making progress. Wasn't he? Oh, man, he just had to be.

But Maggie was so…so fierce about the jinx, was determined not to fall prey to the belief that she could be the one to prove it untrue, to break the long cycle of disastrous marriages in the Jenkins family. No, she had said. No.

And little victories meant nothing if he didn't win the final battle. He couldn't bear that thought. He'd just keep on as he was, chipping away at that wall of Maggie's. He was going to conquer the demon that held her so tight.

He was going to marry Maggie Jenkins. She loved him, he believed that with every fiber of his being. And heaven knew that he loved her. That love would grow, become stronger, unbeatable, smash the jinx into dust to be blown into oblivion.

Luke nodded decisively, snapped off the lamp, then settled close to Maggie, his head on the same pillow as hers just as he'd promised.

But it was many hours before he finally slept.

Two weeks later Maggie and Luke stood in the honeymoon suite on the top floor of one of Phoenix's exclusive hotels.

"Luke, this is awful," Maggie said with a burst of laughter. "A heart-shaped bed? A color scheme of bright red? Velvet spread, upholstery, even the drapes? A shiny red hot tub? It's so tacky, it's beyond belief."

"Oh, I don't know," Luke said, grinning, "I guess it depends on how you feel about red. This place could sure turn a guy off Valentine's Day. Man, they went nuts in here."

"The manager said it's very popular," Maggie said, shaking her head. "That's a scary thought."

"Yep," Luke said, glancing around. "It's even worse than the one that had forty-two stuffed toy cupids. I counted them, you know, and there were actually forty-two of those chubby little guys ready to shoot arrows. That was a nightmare waiting to happen."

"Well, cross this one off the list of possibilities." Maggie looked at her watch. "I've got to rush. I'm meeting Janet and Patty at the bridal shop for the first fitting of their bridesmaids' dresses."

"Have you…um…looked at wedding dresses yet?" Luke said, sliding a glance at her.

"No, not yet. I'm sure the perfect dress for…for Precious is there because the selection is wonderful. That shop is where Ginger got her gown. They're terribly expensive, though."

"No problem," Luke said. "Don't even think about the money. The sky is the limit…or whatever. In other words, go for it."

"Right. Let's get out of here. All this red is giving me a headache."

"Are you sure you can't come to my place tonight?" Luke said as they started toward the door.

"No, I've got to go see my mother, Luke. You know, have dinner with her, chat, what have you. She's feeling neglected and I don't blame her. I haven't been to her house in far too long. I'll just go straight home from there."

"I'll miss you," he said. "I'm getting very spoiled having you next to me in my bed at night and seeing you when I open my eyes in the morning. It's nice. It's more than nice."

Maggie gripped the doorknob, then hesitated and smiled up at Luke.

"Yes," she said, "I agree. It's very, very nice." She laughed. "By the way, you know that superstition you laid on me last night? I want you to know that I purposely put on my left shoe before my right one this morning and I have not had one bit of unluck, if there is such a word."

Luke braced his hand flat on the door to prevent Maggie from leaving the brilliant-red suite.

"Well, now, aren't you turning into a risk taker?" he said, smiling.

"Not really, Luke. I mean, after all, these are just superstitions that I'm declaring to be untrue. You should be feeling a step-by-step sense of freedom as each one gets checked off your list. I don't think I'm taking any risks by doing that."

"Interesting," he said, frowning thoughtfully. "So you're saying that superstitions, old wives' tales, jinxes are based on a foundation of long-standing foolishness."

"Well, no, not entirely. I was referring to superstitions only. There are certain jinxes that have proven merit."

"So you say," he said thoughtfully. "Or could it be rather a long string of poor judgment? I had this friend in college who was convinced he was jinxed when it came to owning a car. Every used vehicle he purchased turned out to be a lemon. So he quit, gave up, said never again. He rode a bike, took buses and taxis. Man, what a hassle."

"But smart," Maggie said decisively.

"I didn't go with that theory. I convinced him to try one more time, run that risky risk. We went to a used-

JOAN ELLIOTT PICKART 151

car lot and he looked at a bunch of vehicles, then settled on the one he would buy if he was going to, which he wasn't. We took it for a test drive and stopped to see another buddy of mine who was a mechanic."

"And he said the car was a clunker. Right?" Maggie said.

"No, he declared it to be prime, good for another hundred thousand miles, so my friend bought it."

Maggie blinked, then frowned. "Really?"

"Really. The last time I saw him he was still driving that thing. He said it gave him cold chills to dwell on the narrow existence he would have had if he hadn't sucked in a deep breath that day and taken that risk, bought the car."

"But—"

"Think about it." Luke dropped a quick kiss on Maggie's lips. "Come on, let's go. You'll be late for the appointment for the dresses."

"The what?" Maggie said absently. "Oh! The dresses. I've got to dash."

They left the suite and as Maggie hurried down the hallway in front of Luke, he punched one fist in the air.

Yes! he thought. He'd scored some points—big-time. The story he'd made up about the guy and car was genius-level thinking, especially since he had done it on the spur of the moment because the opportunity had been so perfect for it.

Maggie had heard every word he'd said, was digesting it in that mighty little mind of hers as evidenced by the fact that she'd momentarily forgotten about the appointment she was almost late for.

He was folding his tent graciously and without complaint each time she declared one of his superstitions, albeit fictitious ones, as nonsense. All he was asking of her was to give up one jinx. One.

The one that would mean the difference between their having a future together or not. The one that would determine their entire lives. The one he had to defeat in the ongoing battle he was conducting to win the war and a forever with Maggie Jenkins.

"I'm just going to tape this hem in place for now," the seamstress said to Maggie, "until the actual bridesmaid is here for the final fitting."

"Oh, I wish it was really me," Janet said wistfully as the seamstress worked on the hem. "This dress is scrumptious. I love this color of green, Maggie. I want to own this dress."

"That's what Patty said before she left," Maggie said, laughing. She was seated on a velvet-covered chair, sipping a cup of tea. "She said this whole business is pure torture because she's had the dress on but it really belongs to someone else."

"She's right," Janet said.

"All set for today," the seamstress said, getting to her feet. "Let me help you take this dress off."

"No, I want to keep it," Janet said, then laughed. "Would it do me any good to throw a tantrum?"

"I'm afraid not," the woman said, smiling.

The dress was removed and the seamstress left the room. Janet began to pull on her own clothes.

"Janet," Maggie said quietly, "may I ask you something?"

"Sure."

"When you married Roger, did you believe that you would be the one to break the Jenkins Jinx, end it for all time?"

"Truthfully?" Janet said, sitting down next to Maggie. "I loved Roger so much, Maggie, that I blatantly ignored things about him that were red-alert signals indicating problems down the line."

Maggie set her teacup on the delicate table next to her and sat up straighter in her chair.

"Really?" she said. "I didn't know that."

"No one did," Janet said, sighing. "I thought I could change him, dum-dum that I was. He gambled far too much, hadn't held a job longer than a year in his entire life, thought money should be spent and enjoyed now with no thought given to the future.

"Even after the babies started coming he didn't get his act together. It was like having another child to raise. When I got divorced, no one asked me why, really. The family just assumed it was the Jenkins Jinx doing its thing."

"And Bill?" Maggie said, her heart racing. "What about your marriage to Bill?"

"Oh, sweetie, that was a joke. I was lonely, broke, scared to death of being a single mother, living paycheck to paycheck, and I latched onto Bill. Six months later I was sick to death of him cheating on me. Ta-da. Divorce number two for Janet the dunce."

"Why…why didn't you ever say that the Jenkins Jinx didn't have anything to do with your divorces?" Maggie said.

"It was easier that way, Maggie. Why tell everyone that I had such lousy judgment, had made such awful mistakes and was paying the price? The whole family felt so sorry for me because I was another victim of the jinx, so I let it stand, kept my mouth shut."

"Don't you believe there really is a Jenkins Jinx?" Maggie said, hardly breathing.

"I honestly don't know," Janet said, frowning. "Is it real? Does this family just have poor judgment in its choice of partners? Or did some of those marriages in our family tree collapse due to the jinx? I don't know the answer to that." She cocked her head slightly and studied Maggie. "Why are you asking me all this? It has been ages since you and I have talked about the jinx."

"I, um. Well, because… Yes, because of Roses and Wishes. I deal with happy brides all the time and…Mom thinks I made a mistake starting a business that only emphasizes what I'll never have because of the jinx. She really believes the jinx is true, you know. Having Roses and Wishes has made me think about it more than I normally would that's all."

Janet narrowed her eyes. "You never could lie worth a damn, Maggie Jenkins. Something is going on with you. Talk to me, little sister."

Maggie got to her feet. "There's nothing to tell you, Janet." She looked at her watch. "My, my, look at the time. I've got to go. I have so much to do. Details, details, details—the list is endless for a wedding."

"*Your* dream wedding," Janet said, rising. "That's what you're tending to."

"Well, it just worked out that way because of this unusual situation with Precious and Clyde," Maggie said. "I explained all that to you. So, yes, this is the wedding I would have if I was going to have a wedding, which I'm not because of the jinx…which you're now suggesting might not be real and…" She slapped one hand onto her forehead. "I'm getting a roaring headache, thank you very much."

"Maggie, there is no way to prove that the jinx is real, no matter what Mom says."

"But we've believed it ever since we were young girls, Janet. We can't pretend it isn't there. We lost count of the divorces in our family tree. There is not one happy Jenkins marriage in our history."

"And there could be an explanation for every one of those divorces just as there is for my two. As for Mom and Dad? The jinx? Come on, Maggie, it was a classic case of the guy who falls for his sexy secretary and thinks he can recapture his youth by dumping his wife and three kids and going off with a bimbo. That's not a jinx, that's a hormone rush or whatever."

"But—"

"I don't know," Janet said, throwing up her hands. "Someday maybe a Jenkins will stay happily married for fifty years and this jinx thing will be old news. Love is powerful when it's right and real. Will that Jenkins be one of my kids? Or will that someone be…you?"

"Me?" Maggie said, her voice a strange-sounding squeak. "Don't be silly. I'm not brave enough to test out the theory that the jinx might not be real. I'm not going to run the risk of having my heart broken to pieces. Nope. Not me."

"Oh?" Janet said, raising her eyebrows. "What happens if you fall head over heels in love?"

I already have, Maggie thought dismally. *And I'm not going to do one thing about it beyond accepting the fact that my time with Luke St. John is measured on the calendar.*

"Let's change the subject," she said. "Want to hear something funny? There's a superstition that when you see an ambulance you'll have bad luck unless you pinch your nose until you see a black or brown dog."

Janet laughed. "That's the silliest thing I've ever heard."

"I know. Try this one. If you have a goldfish in a pond at your home it's good luck, but a goldfish kept inside the house is bad luck."

"Where are you getting this stuff?" Janet said, shaking her head.

"And if the bottom of your feet itch," Maggie rushed on, "you're going to make a trip."

"I'm going to make a trip home right now," Janet said, smiling, "before you lay any more cuckoo stuff on me. Superstitions are nonsense."

"Are jinxes?" Maggie said, suddenly serious. "Is the

Jenkins Jinx as nonsensical as the superstitions I just rattled off?"

Janet sighed. "I don't know. I really don't know. Someone in this family is going to have to fall in love, listen to their heart for the truth, the honest-to-goodness truth of that love and— Good grief, look at the time. I've got to pick up the kids." She gave Maggie a quick hug. "Thanks for letting me play Cinderella in that gorgeous dress. 'Bye."

"'Bye," Maggie said, then sank back down on the pretty chair and stared into space.

Her mind was a mess, she decided. For as long as she could remember she'd believed that the Jenkins Jinx was real. But now? After discussing it with her sister? It was all so confusing, so muddled.

Yes, she was in love with Luke. But, no, she couldn't, just couldn't, run the risk of ignoring the jinx only to discover that it was a genuine curse that hung over her family. But Janet had said that her two failed marriages had nothing to do with a jinx. But then again...

"Excuse me," the seamstress said, coming back into the room.

"Yes?" Maggie said, relieved to be pulled from her jumbled thoughts.

"Time is passing and that wedding you're coordinating will be here before you know it," the woman said. "Are you going to look at our selection of exquisite wedding dresses today?"

"No, not today," Maggie said, an achy sensation gripping her throat as she got to her feet. "I'm suddenly exhausted, so very tired."

"I understand," the seamstress said. "But you will pick the bride's dress soon, won't you?"

"Yes," Maggie said softly. "I'll do it…soon, I promise. I'll have my Cinderella moment, then take the dress off and…and just be me again."

Just Maggie, she thought. Counting down the days until she said goodbye to Luke and was simply Maggie Jenkins. Alone and lonely.

Ten

During the next month Maggie came to feel as though there were two different people existing in her own body.

One was carefree, happy and deeply in love with Luke, enjoying every moment they spent together.

They ate out often, went to the movies, flew a kite in a grassy field, enjoyed a picnic and canoe ride at Encanto Park, shopped at various malls and attended several interesting lectures at Arizona State University. They cooked together—which was a hilarious disaster—tended to details for Precious and Clyde's wedding. And they made sweet, wonderful love.

The other Maggie was consumed by a breath-stopping chill each time she looked at the calendar and saw the time flying by. Summer had turned into fall, school had started again and Phoenix was buzzing with the success of the ASU football team.

They'd celebrated with a special dinner out when they'd finally reserved the honeymoon suite at the very hotel where the reception was to be held. It was perfect, they'd decided. It was decorated in good taste, had a marvelous view of the city lights, a hot tub in the bedroom area and a fireplace in the living room.

Maggie had told Luke that it would be impossible for Precious and Clyde not to like it, while her heart had ached because the honeymoon suite would not welcome Mr. and Mrs. Luke St. John.

Her life, Maggie thought at one point, gave a whole new meaning to the old phrase of laughing on the outside and crying on the inside.

The seamstress at the bridal shop left message after message on Maggie's answering machine, saying she must choose the wedding dress. Maggie created endless excuses why she couldn't get to the shop, as she was terrified she would weep the entire time. The mere thought of selecting that gown, trying it on while knowing it really wasn't hers, was just more than she could bear.

Ginger and Robert returned with glowing reports of their honeymoon in Greece, and the four of them often enjoyed a night on the town. The newlyweds literally shone with happiness, and Maggie had no choice but to sigh and admit to herself that she was green with envy whenever she saw them together.

When Luke announced that it was bad luck to set an empty rocking chair in motion, Maggie dragged him to a furniture store and gave each rocking chair a gentle push to get it going. They dissolved in laughter, apologized to the frowning saleswoman and beat a hasty retreat.

When October marched in and Halloween costumes were featured in every store, Maggie told Luke—again—that the invitations to Precious and Clyde's wedding had to be selected *now* so they could be printed, addressed and mailed.

"Luke," Maggie said one night as they watched a video in her tiny living room, "you keep saying you'll contact Precious and Clyde about the wording on the invitations, but you don't do it."

"I will," he said, his attention on the television.

"When?" she said. She really had no right to nag him because she still hadn't chosen the wedding dress. But, of course, Luke didn't know that. "Those invitations have to be mailed so the RSVP cards can be returned and I can coordinate the amount of food and drink for the reception." She paused. "Are you listening to me?"

"What?" he said, glancing over at her, then back at the screen. "Sure, I hear you. I'll take care of it. I'll call Precious and Clyde tomorrow...or the next day."

"Promise?" Maggie said.

"Hey, would you look at that car. James Bond has the greatest wheels, I swear. No matter how many times I see these movies, I go nuts for the vehicles. Whoa. That baby can really go."

"Mmm," Maggie said, narrowing her eyes.

"If Detroit ever produced one of those, I'd be the first in line to buy it," Luke went on.

"Luke," Maggie said quietly, "I'm beginning to have doubts about the validity of the Jenkins Jinx."

"Yeah, okay. I'd order my car painted in-your-face-red with chrome so shiny that…" Luke stopped speaking, stiffened, then snapped his head around to look at Maggie. "What? What did you say?"

"Nothing," she said, waving one hand in the air. "I didn't mean to speak aloud. It's just on my mind so much that it popped out before I realized that—"

Luke grabbed the remote, turned off the television, then gripped Maggie's shoulders.

"Say it again," he said. "Please, Maggie, say it again. You're having doubts about… Say the words so I can hear them loud and clear. Maggie, you have no idea how much I need to hear you say those words."

"It has become so confusing," she said, meeting his intense gaze. "Whenever I try to think clearly about the jinx, I feel like a hamster running around in one of those wheels and not getting anywhere."

"Go on," he said, not releasing his hold on her.

"My mother told us about the jinx after my father left us," Maggie said, her voice not quite steady. "I grew up believing in it, especially after we researched our family tree and… But I was talking to Janet about her marriages and for the first time in all these years she said she's not totally convinced there is a jinx.

"Maybe, she said, it's just a whole slew of Jenkinses with poor judgment. Or maybe there is a jinx that forces us to make bad choices, or… Oh, I don't know anymore. Janet feels that all it will take to prove there is no such thing as the Jenkins Jinx is for one of us to fall in love—real love, honest, true and for always love—and live happily ever after."

"Yes, yes. She's right. That's good. Great thinking," Luke said in a rush of words. "You have a very smart sister there."

"She said maybe it would be one of her kids that proved the jinx to be nonsense or perhaps it might be…might be…"

"Might be?" Luke prompted.

"Me," Maggie whispered.

"Maggie, yes, it's you," Luke said, his heart soaring. "Maggie Jenkins, I love you so damn much. I am totally, absolutely and forever in love with you. I want to marry you, have babies with you, wake up every morning and have you be the first thing I see. My wife."

"Ohhh," Maggie said, then sniffled as her eyes filled with tears.

"Maggie, do you love me? Do you?"

"Yes. Yes, Luke, I do, so very much. I didn't want to fall in love with you, didn't mean to, but I did. I'm still worried about the jinx because it's been drummed into my head since I was a little girl. One minute I think I don't believe in it anymore, but then I get so frightened and… I'm such a mess.

"But, Luke, do you know what I hang on to like a lifeline to give me courage? It's you. It's you and your superstitions. Your family has believed in those things you've told me for years and years, yet you're so willing to let them go, run the risk of bad things happening because you put your shoes on wrong or forget to carry your acorn or…

"You're so brave, so strong, so willing to move forward and dismiss those superstitions as nonsense and…"

The color drained from Luke's face and he dropped his hands from Maggie's shoulders.

"If you can have that kind of courage," Maggie said, an errant tear sliding down her cheek, "then I should be brave, too, not hide behind my fears, my belief in the Jenkins Jinx."

"Maggie, listen to me. Okay?" Luke said, his voice raspy. "I have to tell you something. But as you're hearing what I have to say, remember that we love each other. We do. We have a wonderful future together just waiting for us to step up and start living it as husband and wife. Will you do that? Remember that?"

"Yes, all right, but you're suddenly so… What is this thing you have to tell me?"

Luke got to his feet, walked around the small room, then sat back down, taking Maggie's hands in his.

"Maggie, my darling Maggie," he said, looking directly into her eyes, "I never…I never believed in any of those superstitions."

"Pardon…me?"

"I'd never even heard of most of them, had my secretary find them for me on the Internet."

"What? I don't understand."

"I was desperate, don't you see?" he said, giving her hands a little shake. "I didn't know how to get you to demolish that wall protecting you from the Jenkins Jinx.

I thought if you continually witnessed me dumping superstitions that I had supposedly believed in all of my life, you'd come to realize that you could do that with the jinx."

"You didn't believe that having goldfish in the house is bad luck?" Maggie said, her voice rising.

"Ah, Maggie, I had a whole aquarium full of goldfish in my bedroom when I was a kid."

"You—you lied to me? About the superstitions? All this time you've been telling me lie after lie, reciting one superstition after another?"

"They weren't lies, exactly. It was part of a master plan I had to win your love, your heart, to blow the Jenkins Jinx into oblivion so we could be together forever. My father helped me a bit. You know, that night in the pizza place with the acorn and—"

"I don't believe this," Maggie said, yanking her hands free. "What else, Luke? What else did you lie about?"

"I wish you wouldn't use that word," he said, grimacing. "It was a plan. The Plan—in capital letters."

"What else, Luke St. John," she said, her voice ringing with fury.

Luke took a deep breath, then let it out slowly, puffing his cheeks.

"The wedding," he said quietly.

"What wedding?" she said, totally confused.

"Precious and Clyde's."

"What about it? What kind of lies could you possibly tell me about their wedding?"

Luke cringed. "There is no…no Precious and Clyde, Maggie. I made them up. I needed a way to stay close to you after you knocked me over, captured my heart, at Ginger and Robert's wedding. The Plan—I bet you're getting tired of hearing those words—The Plan was for you to coordinate your own dream wedding with me next to you every step of the way.

"Then hopefully you'd fall in love with me, just as I already loved you, and everything would be ready for us to get married just the way you'd always dreamed of."

"That's why you kept hedging about the invitations to Precious and Clyde's wedding," Maggie said, nearly shrieking. "You couldn't ask them about the wording they wanted because they don't exist. And…and…we weren't picking out a honeymoon suite for them it was—"

"For us, don't you see? I wanted our wedding to be perfect for you, exactly what you yearned for. And it will be because you've seen to every detail just the way you want it. I did it for you. Us. You." Luke dragged a restless hand through his hair. "Ah, Maggie, please tell me that you understand that what I did was out of love for you."

"What I understand," she said, getting to her feet and wrapping her hands around her elbows, "is that you are a liar. You are despicable. You made a fool of me. Must have laughed yourself silly when you reported back to your father about the great progress you were making with your ever-famous plan."

"No, it wasn't like that," he said, throwing out his arms. "I had to have something to fight the Jenkins Jinx with because you had it wrapped around you like a fortress. And now you love me. And now you have doubts about there being a jinx on your family and—"

"No, I don't," she said, lifting her chin and ignoring two more tears that slid down her face.

"What?" Luke said hardly above a whisper as he got to his feet.

"I have no doubts whatsoever that the Jenkins Jinx exists, is very, very real, and I am its latest victim," Maggie said, her voice trembling. "I fell in love with a dishonest man, a liar, a schemer, a game player, a damnable *planner.*"

"No! You fell in love with a man who loves you so much he was willing to do anything within his power to win your love in return. Because of your belief in that jinx I had to resort to whatever I could do to accomplish that goal. Lies? No, not really. Well, sort of, but—"

"Get…out," Maggie said, tightening the hold on her arms. "Get out of my home and my life."

"Maggie, no," Luke said, "don't do this to us. Don't send me away. We're in love with each other, can have a wonderful life, have babies, grow old together. The superstitions aren't real, don't exist, and neither does the Jenkins Jinx. You're free to love…me."

Luke drew a shuddering breath and extended one hand toward Maggie. "Please, Maggie?" he said, his voice thick with emotion. "Marry me? Please?"

Maggie's trembling legs refused to hold her for another second and she sank onto the sofa, a sob catching in her throat.

This wasn't happening, she told herself frantically.

Oh, please, this wasn't happening. Luke had been playing games with her, with her emotions, her heart, her... There was no Precious and Clyde? How could people who had become so real to her not even exist? And all those dumb superstitions were part of a nasty, devious *plan* to...

How could Luke do this to her? Live a lie day after day, night after night as they made love? He wasn't remotely close to who she had believed him to be. She was a victim of his duplicity.

And she was the latest victim of the Jenkins Jinx.

"Maggie?"

"Leave...me...alone," she said, then covered her face with her hands.

Luke's shoulders slumped and he dropped his chin to his chest for a long moment before raising his head again to stare at the ceiling in an attempt to gain control of his emotions as an achy sensation gripped his throat.

He'd lost the war, he thought miserably. He'd fought the good fight, won some battles, but the ultimate victory was not his to claim. Maggie was sending him away.

She was once again behind the walls, clinging to the jinx, never wanted to see him again. There was nothing more he could do. The only woman he had ever—would ever—love was not his to have and he now understood what a broken heart felt like. This was the greatest pain, the most chilling loss, he had ever experienced.

"I'm sorry," he said quietly, looking at Maggie. "I never meant to make you cry. I never meant to hurt you.

What I did, I did out of love for you so we could be together forever. But I was wrong. I did it all wrong and I'm so damn sorry." He swallowed heavily. "Goodbye, Maggie."

Luke turned and walked slowly from the room, then down the stairs and out the front door of the Victorian house.

Maggie dropped her hands from her face and clutched them tightly in her lap as she gave way to her tears. She rocked back and forth, hardly able to breathe as the tears flowed and the sobs echoed in the silent room.

She finally shifted and curled into a ball of misery on the sofa, crying until there were no more tears to shed. Her head hurt and her heart ached for all that might have been but would never be.

Exhaustion finally claimed her and she slept fitfully, having taunting dreams of acorns, rocking chairs, goldfish and roses. Roses that died, their petals falling and disappearing into oblivion until there was nothing left.

Nothing.

Eleven

After three days and nights of weepy misery Maggie had had enough of her own gloomy company. On Saturday afternoon she called Patty and asked her if she was free to come over. Patty arrived an hour later, took one look at Maggie's pale cheeks and pink, puffy eyes and demanded to know what was going on.

"Tell all," Patty demanded, plunking down on the opposite end of the sofa from Maggie.

And Maggie told all. She sniffled her way through the tale of Luke's deception, of his diabolical *plan*, the endless string of lies he had told. She confessed her love for Luke and announced in no uncertain terms that she was the latest victim of the Jenkins Jinx.

Patty's mouth dropped open at times and she had to

tell herself to shut it as Maggie went on and on with her story.

"I know I have to cancel all the arrangements I've made for the imaginary Precious and Clyde's wedding," Maggie said, dabbing at her nose with a tissue, "but every time I pick up the phone I burst into tears. I'm a wreck. A mess. I may never recover from this disaster. *And I'm just so sad.*"

"That's very obvious," Patty said, nodding. "Whew. This whole thing is... Wow. Maggie, I don't think you're going to like what I'm about to say, but in my opinion this scheme, plan, whatever, of Luke St. John's has got to be the most romantic thing I have heard in my entire life."

"What?" Maggie said, jumping to her feet.

"Sit," Patty said, pointing to the sofa cushion.

Maggie sat. "How can you say that? Romantic? Ha! There is nothing romantic about lies, Patty. Oodles and oodles of lies. Luke doesn't have a superstitious bone in his body, but he made me believe that he... Romantic? Are you crazy?"

"Slow down. Calm down," Patty said, patting the air with the palms of her hands. "Let's back up here. You and Luke were very attracted to each other from the moment you met. Correct?"

"Well, yes, but..."

"If he had suggested at Ginger and Robert's reception that you two date each other, discover just how far that attraction might take you, you would have refused. Correct?"

"Yes, of course," Maggie said. "Something extremely intense happened between us, and I wouldn't have set myself up to have my heart broken by becoming involved with Luke, then falling prey to the jinx. No. No way."

"And Luke," Patty continued, "smart man that he is, realized that at some point and knew he had to come up with an untraditional way to continue to see you. He was determined to be with you, Maggie, no matter what. Think of the time and energy he spent putting his plan into motion and keeping it going."

"Those lies kept things going, all right," Maggie said, glaring at Patty.

"A hunk of stuff like Luke can snap his fingers," Patty said, deciding to snap her fingers, "and have just about any woman he wants. But he wanted you, Maggie Jenkins, and he worked very hard to get you. That, my dear friend, is romantic to the max."

"But—"

"Oh, Maggie, sweetie, the man is so in love with you it just melts my heart. You left him no choice but to be tricky, do anything and everything to be near you, and it was successful because you fell in love with him, too. And what did you do? You threw him out and declared him to be a jerk, or whatever choice description you nailed on him. You need your head examined."

"How can you say that? Whose side are you on?" Maggie said, nearly shrieking. "I thought you were my best friend, not Luke's. I'm talking about lies here, and deception and—"

"And love." Patty sighed wistfully. "Romantic love. Forever love. Will-you-marry-me love. Love in its purest and most beautiful form and—"

"You're getting gushy and mushy," Maggie mumbled. "Really nauseating."

"Well, what would you call it? Maggie, think about it. Really think about all that Luke did to win your heart. It just blows my mind. Good grief, the man was so desperate and determined he even asked his father to help him in his quest to… Oh, wow."

Maggie frowned and stared into space.

"Are you thinking?" Patty said, leaning slightly toward her.

"Yes, but… Well, he did spend a lot of time schlepping around with me to find the perfect honeymoon suite, despite his busy schedule. And he did memorize all those superstitions so he'd be ready to slip them in where he could. And he did keep telling me to plan the wedding of my dreams, all the details, details, details for Precious and Clyde because—"

"Because he was hoping and praying it would really be your wedding because you would be marrying him," Patty said, nodding. "Now you're getting it. Now you've got to admit that this whole thing is unbelievably romantic."

Maggie flattened her hands on her cheeks. "My gosh, Patty, what have I done? All I heard was that he lied to me, was playing a role to carry out his infamous plan and… In the very next second I was convinced that I had fallen prey to the jinx, was in love with the wrong man and… All I could hear was *what* he had done, not *why* he had done it. Then I tossed him out into the snow."

"That's a stretch," Patty said, laughing. "This is Phoenix, remember?"

"You know what I mean. Oh, Patty, I love Luke so much, and he loves me so much, and because of my life-long fears I lost him. I was so horrible to him, so nasty, so…despicable. It's over. Done. Finished. And I have no one to blame but myself. I'm so dumb."

"Yep," Patty said. "You've got that straight."

"Well, thanks a lot," Maggie said, narrowing her eyes.

"Well, for crying out loud, Maggie, you sit there like you're sentenced to weeping buckets for the rest of your days."

"I am!"

"Fine." Patty got to her feet. "One thing is very clear here."

"It is? What?"

"You don't love Luke as much as he loves you."

Maggie's eyes widened. "How can you say that?"

"Easy," Patty said, shrugging. "I opened my mouth and the words popped right out. What else can I think? Luke knocked himself out to win your heart. *The man made a plan.* You? You're just throwing up your hands and feeling sorry for yourself. He fought for you. You're resigned to going through life with a sinus headache from crying. Nope. You don't love him as much as he loves you. No way."

Maggie jumped up again. "I certainly do. I love him with my whole heart and soul and mind and body and…

Forget the body part, because some things are private. But I love him, Patty. I do. You think I can't come up with a *plan* to try to win him back, get him to forgive me? Well, ha! Just watch me. I'm leaping into action. I am woman. Hear me roar."

"Now we're getting somewhere," Patty said, settling back down on the sofa. "Okay, let's brainstorm. Your whole future happiness—and Luke's, too—is at stake here. Let's take it from the top. Think...*plan.*"

"Damn that plan," Luke said. "I lost the woman I love because of The Plan, which I thought was so terrific, so brilliant."

"I tried to warn you that women are really touchy about duplicity, son," Mason St. John said, shaking his head.

The pair was having lunch at Mason's club at the same time Maggie was pouring out her heart to Patty. Luke had managed to choke down about half of his meal before giving up, his appetite gone.

"Yes, you did warn me," Luke said dully. "But did I listen? No, not me. I just plowed ahead with The Plan and now I'm paying the price. I am one very miserable man. The thought of never seeing Maggie again, not having a future with her as my wife, the mother of my children is... Hell, what a mess."

"Indeed," Mason said, taking the last bite of his lunch. "Dessert?"

"No, thanks. I'm not hungry. And I can't sleep at night and I'm aging before my very eyes. I'm a complete and total wreck."

"Mmm," Mason said, patting his lips with a linen napkin. "Care for some advice from your old man?"

"You actually have some for me?" Luke said, raising his eyebrows. "After the disaster I made of this situation?"

"Yep. My advice is…time. Give Maggie space and time to really think this through. Luke, women can run circles around men in the wisdom department. They think deeper, more detailed and emotionally than we do, God love 'em. Allow her to sift and sort what happened, what you did and why you did it. Be patient and wait."

"How long?" Luke said, his shoulders slumping. "Until Maggie visits me in a nursing home and tells me she still thinks I'm despicable?"

"Now that," Mason said, chuckling, "was funny."

"There's nothing funny about this, Dad. I've lost the woman I love!"

"So it would appear," Mason said, pointing one finger in the air. "But I'm not convinced of that yet. Time, Luke. Space. Patience. That's your new plan."

"The word *plan* should be banned from the English language," Luke said with a snort of disgust.

"Well, that's my advice, son. Oh, and do me a favor. Don't come back to the office this afternoon even though we decided we needed to work on that project we're facing. I don't think I can take any more of your sunshine mood. Go for a walk, take in a movie, get drunk, do something, but spare me."

"Thanks a bunch," Luke said glumly.

* * *

The following week went by so slowly, and Luke double-checked the date with his secretary so often that she was eyeing him warily and he decided he'd better knock it off.

In the early afternoon of the Friday following lunch with his father, Luke sat in his office staring into space, something he'd done a great deal the past few days.

He should fire himself for lack of productivity, he thought. He couldn't concentrate on anything but Maggie and that god-awful final scene in her living room. Time? Space? Patience? So far it was getting him zip. He hadn't heard one word from Maggie, and the knot in his gut continually reminded him he was terrified that he never would.

The intercom on the corner of his desk buzzed and he stared at it for a long moment, toying with the idea of ignoring it. It buzzed again. With a resigned sigh, Luke pressed the button.

"Yes, Betty?" he said to his secretary.

"There's a woman named Patty on the phone for you, Luke. She says that she's Maggie Jenkins's best friend and that it's imperative that she speak with you. Line one."

"Got it," Luke said, his heart racing as he snatched up the receiver. "Patty? Hello. This is Luke. Why are you calling? Is Maggie all right? Has something happened to her? Talk to me?"

"I would," Patty said, laughing, "if you gave me a chance."

"Oh. Yes. Sure. Sorry."

"Nothing has happened to Maggie, per se," Patty said, "except for the fact that she's terribly upset. Unhappy. Miserable. Sad. You know what I mean?"

"Yeah, I know what you mean," Luke said, squeezing the bridge of his nose. "There's a lot of that going around."

"But that's not why I called," Patty went on. "I'm at the bridal salon where Janet and I were fitted for the dresses that were supposedly for Precious's attendants at her wedding. I'm helping Maggie cancel all the arrangements, the bookings and what have you she made for Precious and Clyde, who don't need them because they aren't really real."

"And?"

"Well, the owner of the shop says these two dresses have to be paid for today, can't be canceled because…well, they're dresses just waiting for final fittings. I don't have enough money to pay for them and I know Maggie doesn't. I don't want to upset her more than she is by telling her I hit a glitch here. Do you think you could come down here and settle the account?"

"Of course," Luke said. "It's the least I can do. Give me the address." He paused. "Patty, I love Maggie, I truly do. Do you believe there's any hope of her forgiving me for what I did?"

"Gosh, Luke, I don't know what to tell you. I've never seen her so distraught, so… It's heartbreaking, just heartbreaking. It just breaks my heart because it's so…heartbreaking."

"Oh," he said, sighing. "That's bad. Very bad. Not good. It sounds like time is not doing the job."

"Pardon me?"

"Never mind," he said with another deep sigh. "Just give me the address of that store and tell the owner I'm on my way."

"Thank you, I'll let her know," Patty said. "I have to leave now because I have another appointment, but I'll assure the owner that you'll be here soon."

"I'll settle up with any of the suppliers that charge a fee for canceling orders. Man, I wish things were different. I wish… Never mind. This is all my fault. Call me if you run into problems."

"Okay. Sure. We may all end up eating a whole bunch of white-chocolate miniature roses that were to be in tiny baskets at each place setting at the reception."

"Roses and wishes," Luke said quietly.

"Yes. Well. 'Bye for now."

"'Bye Patty."

When Luke entered the bridal salon, a copper bell over the door tinkled to announce his arrival. A woman's voice came from somewhere in the distance calling out that she would be there in a minute. He wandered around the main area of the lushly decorated shop, his hands shoved into the pockets of his pants. He stopped in the middle of the room and frowned.

This was where an upper-crust bride-to-be came to select her attendants' dresses and to pick out her own wedding gown, he thought. With his damnable plan he'd forced Maggie to come here, make choices for her dream wedding while believing it was all for Precious and Clyde's extravaganza.

The same held true for the honeymoon suite, the menu for the reception dinner, every little detail, like white-chocolate roses in little baskets, that Maggie had had to deal with.

His plan hadn't been brilliant, it had been cruel. He, Luke St. John, was the scum of the earth and didn't deserve to be forgiven. Maggie must have daydreamed about those white-chocolate roses at some point in her life, had been in the process of making them a reality while thinking she would then watch Precious and Clyde's guests gobble up the sweet, pretty treat.

Yeah, he was definitely despicable. There wasn't a chance in hell that his beloved Maggie would forgive him for what he'd put her through, and he didn't blame her, not one damn bit.

"Sorry to have kept you waiting," an attractive woman in her forties said, hurrying toward Luke. "I'm Selina Simone, the owner of this salon. And you are?"

"Luke St. John."

"Ah, yes, Patty said you were coming. I trust you understand why I must be compensated for the dresses that Maggie selected."

"Of course," Luke said. "I'll write you a check. I'd like Patty and Janet to keep them. Could you see to that?"

"Yes, it will be my pleasure. They're gorgeous gowns. Maggie has such splendid taste and she was so excited when we found that exact shade of green she wanted for her—for the Christmas wedding she was coordinating. Well, I'm sure Janet and Patty will enjoy owning the creations."

"Right," Luke said gloomily. "It will be nice to know that someone smiled in the middle of this mess. Is there anything else I need to take care of here?"

"Well, yes, as a matter of fact there is," Selina said. "There are accessories, you see. The satin ribbons for the bouquets and what have you."

"Whatever." Luke nodded. "Sure."

"Would you mind coming into the back with me, Mr. St. John? That's where my records are, and it will be easier for me to check the order forms."

"That's fine. Lead the way."

"Well, I have something to tend to and will join you in a moment. Just go through that door over there and wait, if you would be so kind."

This was pure torture, Luke thought as he crossed the room. Every second he spent in this place pounded home the truth of how difficult all this had been for Maggie, how painful, how…heartbreaking, to borrow Patty's word. Yeah, well, he deserved to suffer, louse that he was.

He entered a medium-size room that had thick rose-colored carpeting. Cranberry-colored easy chairs were arranged in a semicircle in front of a white wicker arch with artificial greenery and flowers woven through it. A large three-sided mirror was on the opposite wall with additional chairs in front of it. Soft, dreamy music was playing.

Man, Luke thought, look at this place. It just got

worse and worse. Maggie had probably sat in one of those chairs and watched Janet and Patty try on the green dresses. The gowns of her dreams that she'd believed would be worn by Precious's attendants.

And a wedding dress? God, had Maggie been forced to select that already, too? Try it on? The wedding gown she'd wear if she was going to be the bride, knowing that Precious would walk down the aisle in it? He should be strung up by his rotten thumbs for what he'd done to his Maggie.

Luke jerked as the music became slightly louder. It was clearly the traditional wedding march.

Why were they playing that now? he thought, beads of sweat dotting his brow. He couldn't take much more of this. Maggie must have heard it at some point in this disaster and… Where was that lady, that Selina woman? He had to get out of here.

He looked frantically around, hoping that Selina Simone would appear, then a motion beyond the pretty arch caught his attention and he snapped his head back to see what it was.

Then he stopped breathing as he stared through the arch, finally taking a shuddering breath as a sharp pain shot across his chest telling him he was desperately in need of air in his lungs.

"My God," Luke whispered, his heart thundering. "Maggie."

She was walking slowly toward him, her fingers laced loosely at her waist. And she was wearing an incredibly beautiful full-length white wedding dress. It was an old-fashioned Victorian style with a high neck and a multitude of seed pearls on the bodice. It nipped in at her tiny waist, and the skirt swept to the floor in soft, luscious satin folds. The gossamer veil brushed her shoulders and was turned back to reveal her face.

And Maggie was smiling.

"Maggie?" Luke said, hearing the gritty quality of his voice.

She continued to approach with the measured steps of a bride walking down the aisle to meet her groom as the wedding march continued to play. She finally stopped in front of Luke and he swallowed heavily as he looked at her.

"Hello, Luke," she said softly.

"You are…" Luke cleared his throat. "Maggie, you are the most beautiful bride I have ever seen." He shook his head slightly. "But I don't understand what—"

"I'll explain," Maggie interrupted. "Let's sit down."

"Yes. Okay."

Maggie settled onto one of the cranberry-colored chairs, smoothing her skirt out around her. Luke pulled a matching chair in front of her and leaned forward, resting his elbows on his knees and tapping his laced fingers against his lips.

"Luke," Maggie said, looking directly into his dark eyes, "I hope you'll forgive me for the horrible things I said to you when you told me about your plan."

"Forgive *you?*" he said, splaying his hands on his knees. "I'm the one who wants to beg *you* to forgive *me* for being so—" he glanced around, then met her gaze again "—so cruel and heartless and thoughtless and for telling you all those lies and… The fact that I was desperate, so afraid of losing you, is no excuse for what I put you through. I thought I was being so clever, so… Maggie, I'm so sorry."

"Well, we're even as far as plans go," she said, smiling at him warmly. "Patty and Selina were in on *my* plan to get you here today."

"Oh?" he said, surprise registering on his face.

"Luke, I overreacted terribly when you told me about Precious and Clyde not being real people, about how you wanted me to organize *my* dream wedding and… All I could hear was that you lied to me, weren't who you had presented yourself to be. All I could hear was that I had made a horrendous mistake by falling in love with you and had become a victim of the Jenkins Jinx."

"No, I—"

"Please, just listen."

He nodded.

"I was feeling so sorry for myself," Maggie went on, "felt betrayed and… But Patty made me realize that what you had done wasn't despicable, it was romantic, it stemmed from your love for me and from your heartfelt desire to marry me and give me the wedding of my dreams."

"Yes, yes, that's it," Luke said, nodding jerkily. "That's why I did it. But it all blew up and I was convinced I'd lost you forever, that you'd hide behind those walls of yours and I'd never be able to get near you again."

"Luke, the walls are gone forever. After I talked with Patty, I went for a long walk and listened to my heart. I came to know that love, true love, forever love, is stronger than any jinx or superstition. I know that what you and I have together will withstand the good times, the bad, in sickness and in health, until death parts us and perhaps even beyond."

"Ah, Maggie," Luke said, his throat tightening. "I love you so much."

"I love you, too," she said, sudden tears filling her eyes. "I worked out a plan with Patty and Selina to get you here so you would see me in this wedding dress, the one I want to wear when I become your wife. I wanted to prove to you that I don't believe in the jinx or any superstition like the groom not seeing his bride in her dress before the ceremony. I wanted to prove to you that I'm free to live, to love, and that I want to spend the rest of my life with you as your wife…if you'll have me."

Luke stood and with hands that were not quite steady grasped Maggie's and eased her to her feet.

"Maggie Jenkins," he said, giving up any attempt to hide the tears shimmering in his eyes, "would you do me the honor of becoming my wife? Will you marry me, Maggie? Please?"

"Yes," she said, smiling through her own tears of joy. "Oh, yes."

Luke dropped her hands, framed her face, then kissed her so softly, so reverently, to seal the commitment to their future together.

Right on cue the music changed to a waltz—*their*

waltz. Luke drew Maggie into his arms and they danced around the room as though floating on clouds, looking directly into each other's eyes, seeing matching messages of greater understanding and forgiveness, of the love and happiness that would be theirs to share for eternity.

Several hours into the wedding reception of Mr. and Mrs. Luke St. John, the newly married couple had made their escape to the honeymoon suite.

"Oh, my," Patty said wistfully, "it was all so beautiful, wasn't it? Including me in this gorgeous dress. Just perfect. Every detail, detail, detail, as Maggie would say. Right down to those delicious white-chocolate roses. What a wonderful couple Maggie and Luke make. And happy? I think they give a whole new meaning to the word."

"Yes," Maggie's mother, Martha, said, "you're right. Seeing them together… Well, let's just say that there will be no more talk of the Jenkins Jinx in this family. Maggie and Luke have broken that nasty spell, I just know in my heart that they have."

"I agree with you, Mother," Janet said. "And I'd say that my cute brother does, too. He's danced all evening with that pretty girl he met here." She paused. "Didn't you love the wedding gifts Maggie and Luke gave each other? A tiny gold acorn on a delicate chain for Maggie, and she had gold acorn cuff links made for Luke. She told me it was their special way of remembering all that took place before this memorable night. Oh, God, that is so romantic I could weep."

"I already did," Patty said, laughing.

"No more jinx," Martha said, "and no more Roses and Wishes. Maggie has officially closed her business." She smiled. "She said that enterprise made all her wishes come true, so she's thinking of opening a baby boutique to see if that will hurry along the first little St. John bundle of joy."

"My goodness," Patty said, her eyes widening. "Does that sound superstitious to you?" She laughed. "Well, rest up, folks, because here we go again."

* * * * *

Silhouette® Desire®

From *USA TODAY* bestselling author

Annette Broadrick

THE MAN MEANS BUSINESS

(SD #701)

When a business trip suddenly
turns into a passionate affair,
what's a millionaire and
his secretary to do once
they return to the office?

Available this January from Silhouette Desire

If you enjoyed what you just read,
then we've got an offer you can't resist!

Take 2 bestselling love stories FREE!

Plus get a FREE surprise gift!

Clip this page and mail it to Silhouette Reader Service™

IN U.S.A.	IN CANADA
3010 Walden Ave.	P.O. Box 609
P.O. Box 1867	Fort Erie, Ontario
Buffalo, N.Y. 14240-1867	L2A 5X3

YES! Please send me 2 free Silhouette Desire® novels and my free surprise gift. After receiving them, if I don't wish to receive anymore, I can return the shipping statement marked cancel. If I don't cancel, I will receive 6 brand-new novels every month, before they're available in stores! In the U.S.A., bill me at the bargain price of $3.80 plus 25¢ shipping and handling per book and applicable sales tax, if any*. In Canada, bill me at the bargain price of $4.47 plus 25¢ shipping and handling per book and applicable taxes**. That's the complete price and a savings of at least 10% off the cover prices—what a great deal! I understand that accepting the 2 free books and gift places me under no obligation ever to buy any books. I can always return a shipment and cancel at any time. Even if I never buy another book from Silhouette, the 2 free books and gift are mine to keep forever.

225 SDN DZ9F
326 SDN DZ9G

Name	(PLEASE PRINT)	
Address	Apt.#	
City	State/Prov.	Zip/Postal Code

Not valid to current Silhouette Desire® subscribers.

Want to try two free books from another series?
Call 1-800-873-8635 or visit www.morefreebooks.com.

* Terms and prices subject to change without notice. Sales tax applicable in N.Y.
** Canadian residents will be charged applicable provincial taxes and GST.
   All orders subject to approval. Offer limited to one per household.
   ® are registered trademarks owned and used by the trademark owner and or its licensee.

DES04R   ©2004 Harlequin Enterprises Limited